KARMA

Marquell DeJournette

dizzyemupublishing.com

DIZZY EMU PUBLISHING

1714 N McCadden Place, Hollywood, Los Angeles 90028

dizzyemupublishing.com

Karma
Marquell DeJournette

First published in the United States
in 2021 by Dizzy Emu Publishing

dizzyemupublishing.com

KARMA

Marquell DeJournette

Karma

2020

INT. WOMEN'S PRISON - DAY - AFTERNOON

Two muscular Prison guards/Correctional Officer in their
late 20s early 30s walking beside, escorting a gorgeous
woman in her mid/ late- 20s down the Prison hallways. With
shackles around her ankles and handcuffs around her wrists.

INT. WOMEN'S PRISON VISITING ROOM - DAY - AFTERNOON

The Prison guards/Correctional Officer escorts the prisoner
into a private visiting room. A mid-40 male veteran
detective is sitting at the table while the guards sits the
woman down.

                    VICTORIA
          Detective.

Sitting in the chair the Detective looks and stares at the
woman.

                    DETECTIVE JONES
          Victoria.

Walking away from the woman in the chair the Prison
Guards/Correctional Officer stands by the door. Detective
Jones continues to stare at Victoria.

                    DETECTIVE JONES
          You're such a pretty girl. You're
          smart, you graduated with honors. I
          don't get it. Why blow it all?

Victoria looks into Detective Jones eyes with anger and
regret.

                    VICTORIA
          Well, I fell in love.

INT. (FLASHBACK) THREE YEARS AGO - COLLEGE STUDENT CENTER
HALL - DAY - EVENING

Young adult Males and females in their early twenties
standing around, talking, laughing, and playing pool in the
game room.

WIDE: COLLEGE STUDENTS LAUGHING, PLAYING POOL, AND TALKING

                    VICTORIA (V.O)
          It was my senior year of college
          some friends and I were hanging out
          playing pool at the student center.
                    (MORE)

                                                  (CONTINUED)

                              VICTORIA (V.O) (cont'd)
                    This was around finals time, so a
                    lot of people were there, but all I
                    could see was one person. His
                    name...was Eric.

A handsome young adult male in his early 20s laughing and
smiling with a group of his peers.

CLOSE UP: ERIC SMILING, TURNS AND LOOKS

Standing with a group of her peers, a beautiful young adult
female in her early 20s turns her head, looks at the young
adult male, and smiles.

CLOSE UP: VICTORIA LOOKING AT ERIC

                              VICTORIA (V.O)
                    He was the sexiest man I ever seen.
                    Once he seen me looking at him I
                    never felt so scared and nervous in
                    my life.

The young adult male walks to the female smiling.

WIDE: ERIC WALKING AND APPROACHING VICTORIA

                              DETECTIVE JONES (V.O)
                    He was your first?

                              VICTORIA (V.O)
                    He was my first...my last...my
                    everything.

INT. COLLEGE STUDENT CENTER HALL - DAY - EVENING

Standing by the pool table Eric flirts with Victoria.

                              ERIC
                    I see you looking at me.

She becomes shy and smiles.

                              VICTORIA
                         (Smiles)
                    And...

Eric laughs, looking at Victoria, leaning on the table. She
looks and responds flirtatiously.

                              VICTORIA
                    I don't know what's funny.

Placing his hand on her shoulder, he continues to laugh.

                              ERIC
                         (Laughs)
                    Calm down.

Flirting with Victoria, gazing into her eyes, he slowly
removes his hand off her shoulder, with a smirk on his face.

                              ERIC
                    I like a woman with a little
                    attitude.

Victoria looks at Eric and smiles.

                              VICTORIA
                    Well...you're going to love me.

INT. / EXT. - CAMPUS BUILDING - OUTSIDE - DAY - AFTERNOON

Two young adult beautiful women early 20s opens a pair of
double doors, stepping outside. Walking around the school
campus they see students walking beside, behind, and in
front of them. They also see other students walking into and
out of buildings as well as laying on the campus lawn.

                              JANICE
                    So, who was that guy you was with
                    last night?

Victoria starts to become frustrated and embarrassed.

                              VICTORIA
                    Don't start Janice.

Janice puts her arm in front of Victoria's chest stopping
her from walking. Standing in front of Victoria, moving her
arm away from Victoria's chest. She persuades Victoria to
answer her question.

                              JANICE
                    Vicki I'm your best friend, you
                    know you got to give me the tea.

They continue to walk around the campus.

                              VICTORIA
                    Okay...Okay...his name is Eric.

Teasing Victoria playfully making gestures Janice smiles.

                                                      (CONTINUED)

                              JANICE
                            (Smiles)
                    Whoooo...Eric.

Feeling a little shy and embarrass Victoria looks around the
campus. Becoming upset she speeds up attempting to walk away
from Janice.

                              VICTORIA
                    See...that's why I don't tell you
                    anything.

Quickly responding with a question Janice laughs. Walking up
and next to Victoria.

                              JANICE
                            (Laughs)
                    What?

Slowing down her pace, looking at Janice, putting her middle
finger up towards her direction.

                              VICTORIA
                    You're just jealous. Hater!

Her cell phone begins to ring. Putting her middle finger
down, she grabs and answers her phone surprised.

                              VICTORIA
                    Hello.

Whispering to Janice.

                              VICTORIA
                            (Whispers)
                    It's him.

Looking at Janice talking on the phone.

                              VICTORIA
                    Yeah, it's me I wasn't expecting
                    you to call me this soon, can I
                    call you back later. Okay, I want.

She laughs flirtatiously.

                              VICTORIA
                    Bye.

Watching her hang up and put away the cell phone, Janice is
shock and surprise.

                         JANICE
          Wait...what? You gave him your
          number? How did I miss that?

Placing her arms by her side, walking in a romantic trance,
she blushes thinking about him.

                         VICTORIA
          Yeah, I couldn't resist, I don't
          know how you missed that, you
          probably was in the bathroom or
          something when it happen.

Turning her head away and back towards Victoria, looking at
her with excitement, Janice sighs asking in a cheerful tone.

                         JANICE
                    (Sighs)
          Probably. So, what did he say?

Victoria smiles and answers nonchalantly.

                         VICTORIA
                    (Smiles)
          Nothing much.

Showing interest in the topic of discussion, Janice ask.

                         JANICE
          So, are you going to call him back?

Nonchalantly shrugging her shoulders, Victoria looks at
Janice and calmly answers.

                         VICTORIA
          I don't know.

Playfully bumping into Victoria's shoulder softly with hers,
in a relax and calm tone Janice says.

                         JANICE
          I think you should call him and go
          out. And have a good time. If the
          date suck at least you get a free
          meal out of it.

They both laugh and smile.

                         VICTORIA
                    (Laugh and Smile)
          Whatever.

INT. RESTAURANT - NIGHT

Eric and Victoria are sitting at the table with plates of
food and cups in front of them.

                    ERIC
          You are so beautiful.

He looks at Victoria. With her eyes on her plate she takes
her fork and pokes a piece of food.

                    VICTORIA
          Thank you.

She stares at Eric.

                    ERIC
          What?

Taking her fork placing it into her mouth.

                    VICTORIA
          Nothing, I'm just glad you asked me
          out.

Watching her chew, he takes a sip out of his cup, then
places the cup back on the table.

                    ERIC
          To be honest with you, I was
          nervous to even talked to you that
          night we met.

Dropping her fork on to her plate shock listening to Eric.

                    VICTORIA
          Really?

Eric smiles and responds.

                    ERIC
          Yeah.

Picking up her fork off her plate. She looks down, then
looks at Eric and smiles.

                    VICTORIA
               (Smiles)
          Well I'm glad you're not shy.

Standing up out of the chair, he leans over the table,
kisses her on her cheek, then sits back in his chair
smiling.

(CONTINUED)

                         ERIC
                    (Smiles)
              Me too.

He picks up his cup, sips his drink, then puts the cup down
on the table. They look at each other and smile with
satisfaction.

INT. (PRESENT) WOMEN'S PRISON VISITING ROOM - DAY -
AFTERNOON

Victoria and Detective Jones are sitting across from each
other.

                         DETECTIVE JONES
                    Eric, sounds like he was smoove
                    fellow.

Closing her eyes, she inhales and exhales.

                         VICTORIA
                    (Inhales, Exhales)
              Yeah, he was smoove...very...
              smoove.

She gives Detective Jones a evil look. Frighten by the stare
he trembles.

INT. (FLASHBACK) TWO YEARS AGO - FITNESS GYM - DAY -
AFTERNOON

Janice and Victoria are in a aerobics class in the back row
following the fitness instructor instructions.

                         JANICE
              I'm glad you was able to get your
              head out of Eric's ass for a
              minute, and come share your time
              with your sis.

Huffing and puffing from the instructor instructions
Victoria speaks out of breathe.

                         VICTORIA
                    (Out of Breathe)
              Girl...whatever, you know how it is
              when you're in love.

Teasing Janice with a gesture. Mimicking the instructor she
side eyes Victoria.

                              JANICE
                    In 'love...pleeeaasssee!!!!!

She looks at Janice sarcastically. Speaking with excitement
in her voice.

                              VICTORIA
                    Stop hating. What's been going on
                    with you? Last time we talk you was
                    telling me about a presentation at
                    work! So, how did it go?

Pausing from the exercise, Janice looks at Victoria and
smiles.

                              JANICE
                    I got the promotion.

Stopping in the middle of a new exercise instruction,
Victoria smiles and hugs Janice.

                              VICTORIA
                    Congratulations, I'm so happy for
                    you.

The Instructor of the class is looking at the participants
giving them aerobic exercise instructions.

                              INSTRUCTOR
                    Now to the left.

Janice and Victoria stop hugging.

                              JANICE
                    Thank you.

They continue to follow the Fitness Instructor intense
exercise instructions looking straight ahead.

                              JANICE
                    So what's been up with you? Have
                    you found a job yet?

Doing the exercise following the Instructor instructions
Victoria responds out of breathe.

                              VICTORIA
                         (Out of breathe)
                    No not yet, I told you Eric doesn't
                    want me to work. He's the bread
                    winner and I take care of the home.

Looking at the participants, the Instructor instructs
another intense exercise move.

                              INSTRUCTOR
                    Now stand straight up.

Extending her arm towards Victoria, stopping her movements,
Janice stands up, stops moving, while looking at her.

                              JANICE
                    Wait, so you're telling me you
                    spend all those years in school to
                    be the next Lois Lane, with
                    Pooperman as your boyfriend, to be
                    a stay at home wife?

Catching her breathe Victoria turns her head towards Janice.

                              VICTORIA
                    Did you say, Pooperman?

Continuing doing the exercise moves, Janice looks at
Victoria.

                              JANICE
                    You know what I mean.

Sitting on the floor the Instructor instructs the class
another exercise move.

                              INSTRUCTOR
                    Now let's sit on the floor.

The whole class sits on the floor including Victoria and
Janice.

                              VICTORIA
                    No, what I'm telling you, I'm in
                    love and I support my man.

Janice turns her head and looks at the Instructor while
sitting on the floor.

                              JANICE
                    Okay.

Standing up the Instructor stops moving, looking at the
whole class.

                              INSTRUCTOR
                    Okay, class that is all for today
                    see you all next week.

INT. VICTORIA AND ERIC'S APARTMENT - LIVING ROOM - NIGHT

Victoria is sitting on the couch watching TV. She hears the
door knob jiggle, looking at the door. Seeing Eric at the
door.

                    VICTORIA
          Hey, baby.

INT. VICTORIA AND ERIC'S APARTMENT - NIGHT

 Eric opens and walks through the door.

                    ERIC
          Hey.

He closes the door with an attitude.

INT. VICTORIA AND ERIC'S APARTMENT - LIVING ROOM - NIGHT

                    VICTORIA
          what's wrong with you?

INT. VICTORIA AND ERIC'S APARTMENT - NIGHT

Standing by the front door, staring at Victoria.

                    ERIC
          Please, don't start.

INT. VICTORIA AND ERIC'S APARTMENT - LIVING ROOM - NIGHT

Confuse at his response she looks at Eric.

                    VICTORIA
          What?

INT. VICTORIA AND ERIC'S APARTMENT - NIGHT

Becoming aggravated with her, walking to the kitchen Eric
sighs.

                    ERIC
                 (Sighs)
          Nothing.

INT. ERIC'S AND VICTORIA'S APARTMENT - KITCHEN - NIGHT

Eric walks in the kitchen. He opens the oven, looks inside
of it, sniffs with his nose for a scent of food aroma, and
yells from the kitchen.

                    ERIC
                (Yells)
          What did you do all day?

INT. VICTORIA AND ERIC'S APARTMENT - LIVING ROOM - NIGHT

Sitting on the couch she yells from the living room.

                    VICTORIA
                (Yells)
          I cleaned a little!

INT. ERIC'S AND VICTORIA'S APARTMENT - KITCHEN - NIGHT

Victoria walks in the kitchen, stands in the door way and
watches him.

                    ERIC
          You didn't think about cooking?

Eric closes the oven door. He stands up and looking at
Victoria with anger in his eyes. She tries to calm him down.

                    VICTORIA
          I didn't know what time you was
          coming home, but I can make you
          something real quick. Just give me
          20 minutes.

Yelling and speaking in an angry tone walking by Victoria
bumping her shoulder against his.

                    ERIC
                (Angry Tone)
          Just forget it.

He walks towards the front door leaving the kitchen.
Victoria turns and chases him.

                    VICTORIA
          Where are you going?

INT. ERIC'S AND VICTORIA'S APARTMENT - NIGHT

Stopping at the door he turns to Victoria and screams.

                    ERIC
             (Angry Tone, Screams)
          To find some food.

While exiting the apartment he slams the door. She stands at
the door watching him slam the door heart broken.

SFX: Door Slamming

                    VICTORIA
          I love you.

INT. WILLIAMS HOME - DAY - AFTERNOON

A man in his mid 50s is sitting on a couch watching a
basketball game on television. The door opens Victoria walks
inside.

                    VICTORIA
          Hi daddy.

He turns his head away from the television to Victoria.

                    MR. WILLIAMS
          Hi honey.

Victoria looks at Mr. Williams.

                    VICTORIA
          Is mom home?

Turning his head back to the television.

                    MR. WILLIAMS
          Yeah she's in the kitchen.

She walks towards the kitchen.

                    VICTORIA
          Whose winning?

Stopping for a moment to watch the television.

                    MR. WILLIAMS
          The Lakers.

Glancing at the television for a brief second, then she
looks at Mr. Williams.

(CONTINUED)

                         VICTORIA
              Boy...boy that LeBron James is
              amazing.

Pantomiming playing basketball while watching the game on
television.

                         MR. WILLIAMS
              Best damn ball player in the
              league.

Walking away from the living room towards the kitchen she
nods her head.

                         VICTORIA
              That he is...that he is.

Exiting out of the living room she hears him yell out.

                         MR. WILLIAMS
              And one! That damn LeBron does it
              again.

INT. WILLIAMS HOME - KITCHEN - DAY - AFTERNOON

A middle age woman is in the kitchen preparing a meal and
humming.

                         MRS. WILLIAMS
                    (Hums)

Victoria enters the kitchen.

                         VICTORIA
              Hi mom.

She walks to the woman. Giving Mrs. Williams a hug and a
kiss on her cheek, she smiles. Mrs. Williams instantly stops
humming.

                         MRS. WILLIAMS
              Hi baby.

Walking away she sits in a chair by the kitchen table.

                         VICTORIA
              What are you cooking mom?

Continuing preparing lunch Mrs. Williams joyfully answers.

                                              (CONTINUED)

                    MRS. WILLIAMS
          A little bit this, a little bit of
          that.

Watching Mrs. Williams preparing lunch, Victoria sits back
in the chair, and smiles.

                    VICTORIA
          Mom, you always cooking something
          up.

Rinsing off the vegetables placing them under the faucet.
Mrs. Williams cuts up vegetables and season the meat for
preparation to cook.

                    MRS. WILLIAMS
          Yeah, you know how I do. What's up
          with you? I haven't seen you in
          awhile.

Victoria sighs loudly.

                    VICTORIA
                 (Sighs)
          Nothing much.

Giving her full attention Mrs. Williams stops cutting and
seasoning the food. She looks at Victoria and smiles.

                    MRS. WILLIAMS
          How are you and Eric?

Moving her head left to right she suddenly feels sad.

                    VICTORIA
          I don't know mom. He's been acting
          weird lately. After all these years
          he never acted this way.

Putting her cooking utensils down Mrs. Williams walks to the
kitchen table. She sits across from Victoria.

                    MRS. WILLIAMS
          How's he acting?

Looking at Mrs. Williams beginning to cry, she covers her
face with her hands.

                    VICTORIA
          He's starting arguments for no
          reason, he's always gone, and he
          barely speaks to me.

Standing up out of the chair Mrs. Williams walks to and hugs
Victoria. She whispers in her ear.

                    MRS. WILLIAMS
          My poor baby,girl...that boy is
          cheating on you.

Pushing Mrs. Williams off her instantly becoming upset and
angry. Speaking in a aggressive tone.

                    VICTORIA
          No he's not.

Disappointed in her actions Mrs. Williams looks Victoria up
and down.

                    MR. WILLIAMS
          Vicki I hate to tell you, but he
          is.

In rage Victoria stands up out of her chair.

                    VICTORIA
          Mom I don't believe you. I know
          Eric, he loves me and I trust him.

Turning away from Mrs. Williams proceeding to walk out of
the kitchen. Quickly grabbing Victoria's arm preventing her
from leaving the kitchen.

                    MRS. WILLIAMS
          Vicki listen to me.

She removes her hand off of Victoria's arm. Shouting in
anger Victoria turns and looks at Mrs. Williams.

                    VICTORIA
          Mom! I don't want to talk about
          this any more.

Changing the topic of discussion Victoria yells from the
kitchen.

                    VICTORIA
               (Yells)
          Dad! Whose winning the game?

INT. WILLIAMS HOME - LIVING ROOM - DAY - AFTERNOON

Yelling from the living room Mr. Williams answers.

                    MR. WILLIAMS
                  (Yells)
            Girl you already know!

INT. WILLIAMS HOME - LIVING ROOM - DAY - AFTERNOON

Mr. Williams sitting on the couch watching television. He
jumps off the sofa with excitement from the basketball game.

                    MR. WILLIAMS
            King James!

EXT. OFFICE BUILDING - DAY - EVENING

Victoria walks out of building with a handsome guy in his
mid 20s.

                    VICTORIA
            You have a goodnight George.

George looks at Victoria and smiles.

                    GEORGE
            You too.

He walks away from the building. Watching George walk away
she smiles standing on the side walk.

SFX: Car Horn

Waiting in the car for Victoria honking the car horn
obnoxiously Eric yells out of the window.

                    ERIC
                  (Yells)
            Hello!

She looks at Eric while walking to the car.

                    VICTORIA
            Hi, honey. How was your day?

Opening the passenger car door, she steps inside, then
closes the door.

EXT./INT. ERIC'S CAR - DAY - EVENING

Eric watches Victoria get inside the car with an attitude.

                    ERIC
          Who was that?

Victoria settles in the passenger seat. Grabbing the seat
belt, she places it across her body.

                    VICTORIA
          Who? George? That's just my
          co-worker.

He stares at Victoria in anger.

                    ERIC
          Do you smile at all your co-workers
          like that?

She tries to comfort Eric by caressing his face with her
hand.

                    VICTORIA
          Babe, I always smile, you know I
          love to smile.

Moving her hand off his face, he turns his head, looking
straight ahead side eying Victoria.

                    ERIC
          Uh...huh.

Eric starts the car and drives off.

INT. RETAIL STORE - DAY - AFTERNOON

Janice and Victoria are looking through clothes checking
price and sizes.

                    JANICE
          What's wrong with you?

Looking at Victoria with a sense of concern.

                    JANICE
          Why are you so quiet?

Victoria stares at the clothes as she browse through the
rack.

                                        (CONTINUED)

                          VICTORIA
                   Nothing.

Placing her hand on the clothes rack stopping and
interrupting Victoria from moving the clothes.

                          JANICE
                   You're lying.

Angry and Aggressively she removes Janice's hand away from
the clothes rack.

                          VICTORIA
                   I don't want to talk about it.

Her body jerks in fear from Victoria's reaction.

                          JANICE
                   Okay, we want.

Continuing looking at the clothes, grabbing a shirt off the
rack, Janice look inside the shirt, reads the tag, and check
the size of it. Pausing from browsing through the clothes,
calming down, looking at Janice, nervously Victoria
continues to browse through the clothes.

                          VICTORIA
                   My mom told me the other day, she
                   think Eric is cheating on me.

Examining the shirt, Janice begins to hum.

                          JANICE
                        (Hums)

Annoyed, listening to Janice humming, Victoria stops, and
grunts.

                          VICTORIA
                        (Grunts)
                   What?

Hanging the shirt back on the rack, she turns and looks at
Victoria.

                          JANICE
                   No matter what I say, you're the
                   one that's in love with him. So
                   don't worry about what your mom
                   told you, or what I think.

Taking a deep breathe, backing away from the rack of
clothes, Victoria folds her arms, looking at Janice.

                         VICTORIA
                  What do you think?

Putting her hand on Victoria's shoulder, with a stern look
she answers.

                         JANICE
                  I think you need, to figure out
                  what type of man you're dealing
                  with.

Dropping her head down, feeling sad and depress, she sobs
and cries.

                         VICTORIA
                  Janice I love him.

Wrapping her arms around Victoria, hugging her tightly she
whispers.

                         JANICE
                       (Whispers)
                  Vicki, go find the truth.

They both slowly put their arms to their sides. Janice turns
away from Victoria, resuming browsing through the clothes
rack. Excited seeing a shirt and a pair of pants of her
liking, quickly grabbing them of the rack she smiles.

                         JANICE
                       (Smiles)
                  I'm going to try on these.

She walks away from Victoria and the clothes rack. Victoria
stops crying moving her head left to right smiling, watching
Janice leave.

INT. VICTORIA AND ERIC'S APARTMENT - NIGHT

Victoria enters the apartment.

                         VICTORIA
                  Babe, are you home?

She close the door, place the house keys on the table, then
walks and yells throughout the apartment.

                         VICTORIA
                       (Yells)
                  Babe! Babe! Babe!

Opening the bedroom door, she walks into the room.

INT. VICTORIA AND ERIC'S APARTMENT - BEDROOM - NIGHT

Victoria walks inside the bedroom.

                    VICTORIA
          Babe.

She hears running water in the bathroom. Walking towards the
bathroom door, she sees the door crack.

                    VICTORIA
          Babe.

Eric yells from the inside of the bathroom.

                    ERIC
               (Yells)
          Yeah!

Yelling back at Eric slowly walking away from the door.

                    VICTORIA
               (Yells)
          Oh, nothing I was just seeing if
          you was home!

He yells again.

                    ERIC
               (Yells)
          Oh!

Victoria sees Eric's phone on the bedroom dresser. She walks
towards the phone, grabs it, and begin to read his text
messages. Seeing and alarming text message from a anonymous
woman.

INSERT SHOT:

                    MESSAGE FROM WOMAN
               Hey baby, I can't wait to see you
               again, I had a great time the other
               night. Coco is missing, Mr. Hershey
               bar.

REACTION SHOT:

Reading the text message in rage.

                    VICTORIA
               I can't believe this shit.

Victoria hears the water from the bathroom being turn off.

(CONTINUED)

Sfx: Bath Tub faucet knobs squeaking

Quickly putting the phone down, she quickly jumps in the
bed. He enters the room with a towel wrapped around his
waist.

>   ERIC
>   Hey babe, you're going to bed? It's
>   early.

She turns and looks at Eric.

>   VICTORIA
>   I'm really tired.

Grabbing clothes out of his closet, he starts to get dress,
putting on one clothing material at a time.

>   ERIC
>   Oh okay, I'm going to Smitty's and
>   watch the fight.

Watching Eric get dress, she captures a glance at his phone
on the dresser.

>   VICTORIA
>   Okay.

Finishing getting dress, he quickly grabs the phone off the
dresser.

>   ERIC
>   Call me, if you need me.

He exits the bedroom.

>   VICTORIA
>   Love you.

Victoria begins to cry into her pillow.

INT. JANICE'S APARTMENT - KITCHEN - NIGHT

Janice, Victoria and two other ladies in their mid/late 20s
are sitting around a table, counter, and kitchen island with
glasses of wine in their hands laughing and giggling.

>   KEISHA
>   Girl...I needed this I've been
>   having a tough week.

Keisha sips her wine Janice watches and responds.

                          JANICE
                    Tell me about it.

Seeing Victoria has a sad depress look on her face in a
concerning tone Janice ask.

                          JANICE
                    Vicki! What's wrong?

Victoria has a depress and angry look on her face.

                          VICTORIA
                    Nothing.

Gwen stares at Victoria.

                          GWEN
                    Girl sip that wine and cheer up.

She sips her cup of wine looking at Gwen, Janice, and
Keisha.

                          VICTORIA
                    I got a question? What would you do
                    if you saw some messages in your
                    boyfriend's phone from another
                    woman? Hypothetically speaking.

Sipping her wine Keisha looks at Victoria, moving the cup
away from her mouth, she puts it on the table.

                          KEISHA
                    Kill his ass.

Janice quickly looks at Keisha shock by her comment.

                          JANICE
                    Now, C'mon Keisha.

While sipping her wine Gwen laughs. Sitting closer to Keisha
interested in her comment Victoria interrupts and ask.

                          VICTORIA
                    How would you kill him?

Shock by Victoria's question, quickly looking at her with a
stun look.

                          JANICE
                    Vicki.

Victoria looks at Janice then looks at Keisha.

                         VICTORIA
              Janice, I want to hear, what she
              has to say. Go ahead Keisha.

Keisha acts like she's cutting and shoving an object.

                         KEISHA
              I don't know, I probably cut his
              little thing off and put it in his
              mouth. For all the lies he has
              told.

Putting her hand on her chin Victoria is intrigued listening
to Keisha.

                         VICTORIA
              Really now.

Getting upset with the topic of conversation Janice shouts
in front of everybody.

                         JANICE
                   (Shouts)
              Can we please stop talking about
              killing people!

Frighten by Janice's reaction Keisha responds calmly.

                         KEISHA
              Okay.

Looking at all three ladies Gwen speaks nonchalantly.

                         GWEN
              I'm with Keisha I will kill his
              ass.

In frustration Janice looks at Gwen.

                         JANICE
              Gwen!

Shrugging her shoulders Gwen looks at Janice.

                         GWEN
              What? I'm just saying.

She nonchalantly sips her wine.

INT. JANICE'S APARTMENT - LIVING ROOM - NIGHT

Janice, Victoria, Keisha, and Gwen are laughing and giggling sitting on the sofa. Keisha looks at Victoria, Janice and Gwen.

> KEISHA
> Okay, ladies I have a big day
> tomorrow, so I'm going to go ahead
> and head home.

Gwen and Keisha gets off the sofa and stands up.

> GWEN
> Me too.

Watching Keisha and Gwen stand up, Victoria stays seated, Janice stands up and walks Gwen and Keisha to the front door.

INT./EXT. JANICE'S APARTMENT - FRONT DOOR - NIGHT

> JANICE
> Okay, ladies good night.

Keisha hugs Janice at the front door.

> KEISHA
> Night.

After Keisha stops hugging Janice. Turning to Gwen, looking at her, leaning toward her, reaching out Janice attempts for a hug. Gwen and Janice hugs each other at the front door.

> GWEN
> Night.

Once they stop hugging Keisha and Gwen exits.

Sfx: Door closing

INT. JANICE'S APARTMENT - LIVING ROOM - NIGHT

Hearing Victoria crying Janice walks away from the front door and rushes to living room.

> JANICE
> What's wrong Vicki?

Victoria looks at Janice with tears coming down her eyes.

(CONTINUED)

                         VICTORIA
                    Eric is cheating on me.

Getting upset Janice paces back and forth, then stops in the
middle of her sentence.

                         JANICE
                    That son of a...wait now I see why
                    you ask that question earlier.

Wiping the tears off her face, Victoria sniffs, wipes her
nose, then drops her head in embarrassment.

                         VICTORIA
                    Yeah. I don't know what to do, I
                    love him so much.

Janice sits next to Victoria, wrapping her arms around her
shoulders.

                         JANICE
                    But, he doesn't love you. Look, you
                    need to kick his ass to the curb.
                    They're plenty of men out there
                    move on.

With tears in her eyes Victoria looks at Janice.

                         VICTORIA
                    I don't want no other man, I want
                    Eric to want me as much as I want
                    him.

Placing her hand near Victoria's face, Janice wipes the tear
off her eye. She comforts Victoria by hugging her.

                         JANICE
                    I know you do.

As Victoria stops crying. Looking at Janice, speaking in a
concern tone she ask.

                         VICTORIA
                    So, what do I do?

Extending their arms, giving each other separation, putting
their arms by their side, Walking away from Victoria to a
counter with two glasses and a bottle of wine on top of it.
Janice grab the two glasses and bottle of wine off the
counter top.

                              JANICE
                    You're going to have to figure that
                    out.

Returning with the bottle and two glasses in hand Janice
sits next to Victoria. Opening the bottle of wine, she puts
the glasses on a table top and pours the wine into the
glasses.

                              JANICE
                    Until you do, drink this and if
                    that's not enough I have more.

She stops pouring and hands one of the glasses to Victoria.

                              JANICE
                    Where going to get through this,
                    and that motha fucka will pay
                    believe it, because Karma is a
                    bitch.

Grabbing her glass of wine.

                              VICTORIA
                    This is True.

Victoria wipes a tear off her eye.

                              JANICE
                    I got your back.

Looking at Janice, Victoria smiles.

                              VICTORIA
                    Thanks Sis.

They toast their glasses.

                              JANICE
                    I love you.

Both smiling at each other.

                              VICTORIA
                    Love you too.

CLOSE UP: OF GLASSES TOUCHING EACH OTHER

INT. VICTORIA AND ERIC'S APARTMENT - KITCHEN - DAY - EVENING

Eric is looking around the kitchen for food in the
refrigerator and stove. He yells for Victoria.

                    ERIC
              (Yells)
          Victoria!

Victoria walks into the kitchen.

                    VICTORIA
          Why are you yelling.

Looking at Victoria with anger, he yells and speaks
aggressively.

                    ERIC
              (Angry)
          How come you didn't cook or go
          grocery shopping. I am starving in
          this shit hole!

She looks at Eric with an attitude.

                    VICTORIA
          First of all, this is our home a
          place we build a relationship in, a
          place where we started our lives as
          a couple in, a place where we
          sleep, and eat. This is not a shit
          hole. Second of all you were
          suppose to go grocery shopping.

Beginning to walk away from Eric, quickly grabbing her arm
aggressively stopping her movements he screams.

                    ERIC
              (Screams)
          Don't you walk away from me. I'm
          talking to you!

Becoming fearful of Eric trembling nervously she turns her
head to look at him with a tear in her eye.

                    VICTORIA
          Eric let me go.

He grabs her arm tighter.

                    ERIC
          What are you going to do. Uhh...

(CONTINUED)

With fear in her eyes looking at Eric, crying in pain
Victoria pleads.

                    VICTORIA
          Please...Eric let me go.

Laughing looking at Victoria, slowly he removes his hand off
her arm.

                    ERIC
              (Laughs)
          I'm not going to hurt you.

Shock by Eric's actions, staring at him in disbelief
Victoria whispers.

                    VICTORIA
              (Whispers)
          Who are you?

Eric looks Victoria up and down with a frown on his face.

                    ERIC
          What does that suppose to mean? I
          don't have time for this shit. I'm
          going to get me some food. You stay
          in this shit hole and starve.

He exits out the front door Victoria stands and watches him
walk away confuse.

Sfx: Door Slamming

                    VICTORIA
          I love you.

A tear falls down her eye.

INT. VICTORIA AND ERIC'S APARTMENT - BEDROOM - DAY - EVENING

Phone Rings. Victoria is lying on the bed crying.

                                              INTER CUT

INT. WILLIAMS HOME - DAY - EVENING

Mrs. Williams sitting on the couch watching TV with her
phone on her ear.

INT. VICTORIA AND ERIC'S APARTMENT - BEDROOM - DAY - EVENING

Answering the phone crying Victoria speaks in a soft and low
tone.

                    VICTORIA
               (Crying)
          Hello.

Hearing Victoria crying on the phone made Mrs. Williams
worry and question.

                    MRS. WILLIAMS
          Vicki...Vicki baby, what's wrong?
          Why are you crying?

Sitting up on the bed wiping her tears from her eyes
Victoria gradually stops crying.

                    VICTORIA
          No reason momma. What's up?

Becoming concern, glancing at her phone confuse by
Victoria's response in a worrying tone Mrs. Williams ask.

                    MRS. WILLIAMS
          Are you sure?

Wiping a tear off her eye, slowly speaking in a soft tone
Victoria answers.

                    VICTORIA
          Yes.

Mrs. Williams gets off the couch and walks to the Kitchen.

                                        INTER CUT

INT. WILLIAMS HOME - KITCHEN - DAY - EVENING

Walking inside the kitchen, she walks to the kitchen
counter, and grabs a snack off it with the phone to her ear.

                    MRS. WILLIAMS
          Okay, you know I'm here for you
          baby. If something is wrong.

                                        INTER CUT

INT. VICTORIA AND ERIC'S APARTMENT - BEDROOM - EVENING

Smiling with joy Victoria wipes a tear off her cheek.

                    VICTORIA
          Yes momma I know. You always got my
          back.

Laughing and smiling Mrs. Williams begins to eat her snack.

                    MRS. WILLIAMS
          And you know that.

They Both laugh at the same time.

                    VICTORIA
          I love you Momma.

Slowly chewing and swallowing her snack Mrs. Williams stops
eating, pauses, and ask.

                    MRS. WILLIAMS
          I love you to baby. Hey are you and
          Eric still coming over Sunday for
          dinner?

Depress answering the question.

                    VICTORIA
          I don't know momma, I haven't
          mention it to him yet.

                                        INTER CUT

INT. WILLIAMS HOME - DAY - EVENING

Mrs. Williams walks back to the couch with her snack in her
hand. She sits on the couch and begins to eat it.

                    MRS. WILLIAMS
          Okay, well let me know by Saturday
          night. Your father and I can make
          other plans. You know it's been
          awhile since your mom tasted that
          cucumber.

Licking her lips laughing through the phone.

                                        INTER CUT

INT. VICTORIA AND ERIC'S APARTMENT - BEDROOM - DAY - EVENING

Pantomiming and making vomit noises through the phone
Victoria shakes her whole body in disgust.

                    VICTORIA
          Mom, that's disgusting.

Giggling with snack in hand making gestures Mrs. Williams
responds quickly.

                    MRS. WILLIAMS
          Girl, just give me a heads up.

Victoria laughs and smiles.

                    VICTORIA
          Okay.

Getting excited watching Mr. Williams walk inside the house
Mrs. Williams makes flirtatious noises with her mouth while
looking at him close the front door.

                    MRS. WILLIAMS
          Your father just walked in the
          house. Talking bout it got my mouth
          watery. I got to go.

Disgusted listening to Mrs. Williams.

                    VICTORIA
          Ewww. Bye Ma.

Laughing through the phone Mrs. Williams speaks in a
compassionate tone.

                    MRS. WILLIAMS
          Love you.

Happily smiling exhaling in relief Victoria leans back and
lays on the bed.

                    VICTORIA
               (Exhales)
          Love you too.

Sitting on the couch, looking and yelling toward Mr.
Williams direction, quickly moving the phone away from her
ear.

                    MRS. WILLIAMS
          Baby! bring that cucumber over
          here. I got a taste for some salad.

(CONTINUED)

Yelling through the phone Victoria hurries and rushes off
it.

                    VICTORIA
                 (Yells)
          Ma!

Mrs. Williams and Victoria end the phone call.

EXT. PARK - OUTSIDE - DAY - AFTERNOON

Janice and Victoria both are sitting on the city park bench
watching people walk and jog by them.

                    JANICE
          What's been going on girl?

Victoria looks at the ground. She turns her head slowly,
looking at Janice, with watery eyes.

                    JANICE
          Girl, What's wrong?

Putting her head on Janice's shoulder Victoria starts to
cry.

                    VICTORIA
                 (Crying)
          It's Eric.

Moving closer, wrapping her arm around Victoria's body in a
calm voice Janice questions.

                    JANICE
          What about him?

Maneuvering Janice's arm off her body, becoming angry,
wiping the tears off her eyes, and speaking in aggressive
tone Victoria stops crying.

                    VICTORIA
          Everything, the cheating, the
          disrespect...

Placing her hand on Victoria's shoulder, looking into her
eyes, Janice speaks in angry tone.

                    JANICE
          Did he put his hands on you?

Moving her shoulder away from Janice's hand frustrated with
her question Victoria looks at her confuse.

                                              (CONTINUED)

                              VICTORIA
                    No. Why would you say that?

Janice put her hands up reacting to Victoria.

                              JANICE
                    Whoa! Just asking. You need to get
                    rid of him.

Victoria wipes a tear off her facial cheek. Looking at
Janice, speaking in a calm tone.

                              VICTORIA
                    It's not that easy.

With her hands down to her side making hand gestures Janice
rolls her eyes.

                              JANICE
                    Sure it is. This what you do. You
                    walk up to Eric and say look motha
                    fucka this shit is over. Pack your
                    shit and get the fuck out.

Rubbing her forehead, putting her hands on her face,
Victoria sits back, and sighs.

                              VICTORIA
                         (Sighs)
                    His name is on the lease not mine.

Patting Victoria on the back Janice places her arm around
Victoria's shoulder.

                              JANICE
                    Oh. Well you can pack up your
                    things and come stay with me.

Smiling with excitement Victoria looks at Janice.

                              VICTORIA
                    Are you sure?

Extending her arm away, placing her hands on both of
Victoria's shoulders, in a concerning tone Janice responds.

                              JANICE
                    Vicki you're my sister I got your
                    back. Fuck Eric let him be with the
                    text message bitch.

She removes her arm and hand off Victoria. Slowly standing
up Victoria looks up to the sky.

                                                    (CONTINUED)

                          VICTORIA
              Yeah, you're right he can be with
              text bitch. I don't need him.

Exhaling, looking down at Janice with a smile on her face.

                          VICTORIA
                     (Exhales, Smiles)
              Thanks Janice.

Standing up looking at Victoria with her hands by her side
smiling Janice speaks in a stern voice.

                          JANICE
              You know I got you.

They both look at each other and hug.

INT. VICTORIA AND ERIC'S APARTMENT - NIGHT

Victoria Walks through the door with bags of groceries of
different food items in her hands. Eric is sitting on the
couch watching television.

                          ERIC
              Bout time you made it home.

Walking into the apartment with the bags in her hands
Victoria rolls her eyes.

                          VICTORIA
              Don't start. Can you help me with
              these bags?

He gets off the couch, walks, and approaches Victoria.

                          ERIC
              Better be food, because I'm fucking
              hungry.

Looking through one of the bags that Victoria is carrying,
Eric grabs an apple.

                          VICTORIA
              Why do you have to talk like that?

Taking a bite of the apple Eric looks at Victoria.

                          ERIC
              Like what?

With the bags still in her hands looking at Eric up and down
she sighs.

                                                    (CONTINUED)

                              VICTORIA
                          (Sighs)
                    Just aggressive.

Eric puts the apple back in the bag.

                              ERIC
                    Fuck that, give me the bags.

She hands over the grocery bags to Eric.

                              VICTORIA
                    Thank you.

He grabs the grocery bags with both hands then walks away
from Victoria.

                              ERIC
                    Whatever.

INT. VICTORIA AND ERIC'S APARTMENT - KITCHEN - NIGHT

Victoria and Eric walk inside the kitchen.

                              VICTORIA
                    What's wrong?

Eric places the grocery bags on the kitchen counter.

                              ERIC
                    You left me in here for hours
                    starving. I've been waiting all day
                    for you to bring these groceries.

Frustrated listening to Eric giving him an angry look
Victoria speaks in a stern voice.

                              VICTORIA
                    You are a grown ass man. You know
                    how to order food or better yet go
                    to the store your damn self.

She walks out of the kitchen. Following her to the kitchen
Eric screams.

INT. VICTORIA AND ERIC'S APARTMENT - HALLWAY - NIGHT

                              ERIC
                    Wait, who the fuck, you think you
                    talking to like that?

                                              (CONTINUED)

Stopping in mid step Victoria turns and approaches Eric
aggressively. Poking him in the chest with her index finger.

                    VICTORIA
          Who the fuck you think you are,
          talking to me like that you're not
          my fucking daddy.

Eric grabs her arm squeezing it tightly stopping her from
poking him.

                    ERIC
          Bitch.

Victoria looks at Eric with fear.

                    VICTORIA
          Eric, get your hand off me, you're
          hurting me.

He squeeze her arm tighter.

                    ERIC
          Well you better fucking listen. The
          disrespect has got to stop. Your
          man is home sitting alone waiting,
          his lady is not in sight at all no
          cleaning, no food cook. I thought
          you were the one. You're just a
          free loading bitch. Get the fuck
          out my house.

Removing his hand from Victoria's arm turning his back Eric
walks away from her. Watching him walk away Victoria follows
and chases Eric.

                    VICTORIA
          Eric...no, I love you. Please baby,
          I'll cook, I'll clean, I'll do
          whatever you say I love you.

Beginning to beg and cry Victoria continues to follow Eric.
Feeling the impact of Victoria running into his back Eric
stops walking, turns, looks at Victoria, and points at the
direction of the front door.

                    ERIC
          Just get the fuck out.

Falling to the floor Victoria crawls towards Eric while
crying and sobbing.

(CONTINUED)

                         VICTORIA
                Eric please, after all these years
                your going to throw it away over
                some Co Co bitch.

Eric stares at Victoria and begins to get angry.

                         ERIC
                How do you know about Co Co?

Looking up to him on her knees Victoria yells.

                         VICTORIA
                     (Yells)
                So it's true you are cheating on
                me.

Calmly looking down at Victoria in a relax tone Eric speaks.

                         ERIC
                Well baby she doesn't mean nothing
                to me. She's just a smash and dash.

Listening to Eric feeling unappreciated Victoria screams.

                         VICTORIA
                     (Screams)
                Why are you smashing her at all?

He walks to Victoria, kneels down slowly, grabs her hand,
wipes her tear, stands her up, and looks into her eyes.

                         ERIC
                I got drunk one day at Smitty's
                after we had our first argument.
                She walked up to me and ask me, was
                I single? I was still mad at you I
                told her yeah. And that's how it
                started and it just never stop.

She calmly ask looking at Eric.

                         VICTORIA
                Do she know about me?

With a sad puppy dog look on his face Eric remove his hand
off Victoria's hand.

                         ERIC
                Kind of.

Becoming upset at Eric trembling and shaking Victoria looks
at him with rage.

                                              (CONTINUED)

                         VICTORIA
                What do you mean kind of?

In a calm tone Eric softly answers.

                           ERIC
                It means maybe.

Pushing Eric with both her hands, poking his right pectoral
with her index finger repeatedly out of anger Victoria
yells.

                         VICTORIA
                         (Yells)
                So she knows bout me! And I'm just
                now hearing about her now?

Putting her hands by her side Victoria starts to walk
towards the living room. He reaches out and chases her.

                           ERIC
                Baby wait.

Hearing Eric's voice Victoria stops walking.

                         VICTORIA
                You're right I should leave, you
                don't love me.

She turns and walk towards their bedroom, Eric follows.

                           ERIC
                I do love you, as a matter of fact
                I'm going to cook for you.

Eric grabs her and pulls her to the kitchen.

INT. VICTORIA AND ERIC'S APARTMENT - KITCHEN - NIGHT

Placing her onto a chair Victoria sits crying and yelling at
Eric.

                         VICTORIA
                If you want us to work you have to
                get rid of that CoCo bitch!

Kneeling down on both knees in front of Victoria. He grabs
both her hands with a sensual touch looking up into her
eyes.

                                          (CONTINUED)

CONTINUED: 39.

                         ERIC
              Baby, I promise I want to be with
              you and no one else.

Standing on his feet he walks to the refrigerator grab food
items out of it and some out of the grocery bags.

                         ERIC
              I didn't mean any of the things I
              said earlier I love you and I'm
              sorry for starting shit and that
              CoCo bitch.

Looking at Victoria, standing, eating the food Eric smirks.
Sitting in the chair with red puffy watery eyes Victoria
looks at Eric.

                         VICTORIA
              Just get rid of her and lets get
              back to us. No fighting or
              disrespecting each other. Agreed?

Quickly stop eating, he puts the food down on the kitchen
counter, walks to Victoria, stands her up, wrap his arms
around her, and gives her a huge romantic hug.

                         ERIC
              Agreed.

They both look into each other eyes and kiss. After the kiss
Eric stops hugging Victoria, walks back to the kitchen
counter, and to the bags of groceries. He grabs different
food items out of the bags and begins to prep as well as
cook the food of his choosing. Victoria sits back down in
the chair, smiles, and watches Eric every movement.

INT. NAY NAY'S BEAUTY SALON - DAY - AFTERNOON

Janice and Victoria are sitting in the beauticians chair
with salon capes covering their bodies. Two beauticians are
pampering Janice and Victoria by doing their hair, manicure,
and pedicure.

                         JANICE
              I thought you was kicking bitch boy
              to the curb.

Victoria becomes frustrated with Janice's comment.

                         VICTORIA
              Can you please not call him that?

                                          (CONTINUED)

Reaching out and grabbing a magazine off the beautician counter top Janice flips the pages and starts to read it.

                    JANICE
          What happen to that confident I'm
          going to kick his ass to the curb
          woman at the park.

Watching her reflection Victoria stares at the mirror on the wall.

                    VICTORIA
          I decide to give him another
          chance. That's all.

Becoming upset with Victoria placing the magazine on her lap Janice looks at her in a mean and angry way.

                    JANICE
          Another chance! Why?

Turning her head away from the mirror Victoria looks at Janice.

                    VICTORIA
          Because...

Quickly interrupting Victoria grabbing the magazine off her lap Janice continues to flip the pages.

                    JANICE
          I know...I know I love him, one day
          love is going to run out, then
          what?

Confused looking at Janice, grabbing, and taking away the magazine from her.

                    VICTORIA
          Why do you have be so negative?

Staring into Victoria's eyes Janice speaks with a stern voice.

                    JANICE
          I'm not, I'm being honest and real
          with you. Eric ain't shit he is
          using you he don't love you.

Victoria turns her head back to the mirror.

                         VICTORIA
                Yes he does, Janice.

Grabbing the magazine from Victoria's hand sitting in the
salon chair Janice calmly continues to read it.

                         JANICE
                Okay, wise words from Ruff Ryder's
                first lady and I quote "love is
                blind and it will take over your
                mind, what you think is love, is
                truly not, you need to elevate and
                find, love is blind."

Jumping out of the salon chair Victoria yells in the beauty
shop scaring the two beauticians and other customers.

                         VICTORIA
                  (Yells)
                He loves me and I love him and
                there's nothing blind or deaf about
                that.

Looking around the shop with the magazine in her hand Janice
sees everyone reaction to Victoria. She gets out of the
salon chair to calm her down.

                         JANICE
                I hear you, you know I support you
                and love you. Just be careful.

After Victoria calms down they both sit back in the salon
chairs. Janice continues to flips and reads the magazine.

                         VICTORIA
                Everything is good.

Slowly smiling Victoria watches Janice then looks at the
mirror smiling completely.

INT. ROSE' GOURMET - RESTAURANT - NIGHT - EVENING

Eric and Victoria are sitting at a table with food and
drinks in front of them. A gentleman glances at Victoria
from another table. Watching him looking at Victoria
becoming angry Eric yells and screams at him.

                         ERIC
                  (Yells, Screams)
                What the fuck are you looking at?

Everyone in the restaurant stops their movements and stares at Eric. Looking at Eric feeling embarrass Victoria covers her face from the public with her napkin.

                    VICTORIA
              Stop acting like that.

He looks at Victoria with an emotion of anger.

                    ERIC
              He need to keep his eyes at his
              damn table.

Placing the napkin back on the table Victoria grabs the cup that's in front of her and sips her drink. Putting her cup back on the table she looks at Eric.

                    VICTORIA
              Calm down. Ready to go?

Hearing his phone ring Eric takes it out of his pants pocket. He answers the phone.

                    ERIC
              Hello.

Seeing Eric answering his phone Victoria becomes upset.

                    VICTORIA
              Whose that?

Annoyed by Victoria rolling his eyes Eric rushes off the phone.

                    ERIC
              I'm call you back.

Quickly ending the phone call Eric winks flirting with Victoria.

                    ERIC
              Nobody baby.

Victoria places her arm on the table palms up indicating to Eric to hand over his cell phone to her.

                    VICTORIA
              Well, let me see your phone.

Eric speaks in a aggressive tone.

                              ERIC
                         (Aggressive Tone)
                    Let's not do this in here.

With rage in her eyes Victoria looks at Eric.

                            VICTORIA
                    Fine.

Grabbing their belongings Eric places the money on the
table. They get out of the chairs, walk away from the table,
and exit the restaurant.

EXT./INT. CAR - NIGHT - EVENING

Eric is driving while Victoria is sitting in the passenger
seat looking out the window.

                              ERIC
                    You're not speaking to me now?

Victoria turns and look at Eric.

                            VICTORIA
                    You might not like, what I got to
                    say.

He looks at Victoria then looks at the road.

                              ERIC
                    Just spit it out.

She folds her arms.

                            VICTORIA
                    Okay, let me see your phone.

Moving his head left to right looking straight ahead at the
road annoyed by Victoria's request Eric sighs.

                              ERIC
                         (Sighs)
                    Not this again.

Taking and grabbing his phone throwing it at Victoria.

                            VICTORIA
                    Don't be throwing things at me.

Catching and grabbing the phone with her hands looking down
at it Victoria sees a screen of numbers.

                                              (CONTINUED)

                          VICTORIA
                    What's the code?

Becoming more annoyed with Victoria and her questions Eric
turns his head towards her.

                            ERIC
                    You know the code it's your
                    birthday.

Looking down at the phone Victoria presses numbers on it.

                          VICTORIA
                    Better be.

She scrolls through the phone. He turns his head back to the
road.

                            ERIC
                    See, nothing.

Not finding any evidence of cheating in the phone out of
anger and frustration Victoria throws Eric's phone back at
him.

                          VICTORIA
                    You probably erased it.

Grabbing the phone from his lap Eric quickly looks through
it. Then he puts it down continuing looking at the road.

                            ERIC
                    Erased what?

Victoria rolls her eyes while looking at Eric.

                          VICTORIA
                    Whatever you don't want me to find.

Eric reaches out for Victoria's hand, she quickly moves her
hand away.

                            ERIC
                    Where's the trust?

She gives Eric a mean stare.

INT. VICTORIA AND ERIC'S APARTMENT - NIGHT - EVENING

Victoria and Eric enters the apartment. Eric phone rings, he answers it, then places the phone to his ear.

                    ERIC
          Hello.

Leaning her head and ear next to Eric's, becoming upset watching him answering the phone.

                    VICTORIA
          Whose that?

Speaking in the phone Eric turns his head to look at Victoria.

                    ERIC
          Hold on.

Quickly running to the bathroom for privacy Eric continues his conversation on the phone.

                    VICTORIA
          Eric Where are you going?

Chasing after Eric running behind him yelling and screaming Victoria reaches out. Eric closes the bathroom door in Victoria's face. Angry at Eric for closing the door in her face Victoria knocks on the door repeatedly.

                    VICTORIA
          Eric, Eric, Eric open this door.

SFX: Toilet flushing

Victoria stops knocking on the door. He quickly opens the door.

                    ERIC
          What's wrong baby?

Frustrated with Eric and his actions Victoria stands in the bathroom doorway with her arms folded.

                    VICTORIA
          What the fuck was all that about?

Standing in front of the sink facing forward, turning on the water faucet, grabbing the soap, he puts the soap on his hands, and proceed to wash them.

                                        (CONTINUED)

>   ERIC
>   What are you talking about?

Still standing in the bathroom doorway Victoria watches
Eric. Once Eric finish washing his hands and drying them he
immediately approaches the bathroom doorway and stands in
front of Victoria.

>   VICTORIA
>   Why did you run in the bathroom
>   like that?

Moving away from the doorway Victoria gives Eric walk space
to leave the bathroom. Walking out of the bathroom into the
hallway Eric smirks at her.

>   ERIC
>   (Smirks)
>   Oh, I had to go to the bathroom. Is
>   that okay ma'am?

She follows Eric down the hallway.

>   VICTORIA
>   Don't be funny, let me see your
>   phone?

INT. VICTORIA AND ERIC'S APARTMENT - LIVING ROOM - NIGHT -
EVENING

Eric walks into the living room and sits on the sofa.

>   ERIC
>   Here we go with this shit again.

Victoria walks into living room and stands in front of Eric
with her hand out. Waiting for Eric to hand over his phone
stands with her hand and palms out. He puts his hand in his
pocket and pulls it out. Staring at his phone Eric begins to
press buttons on the keypad. She quickly grabs Eric's phone.

>   VICTORIA
>   Not this time.

Sweating and worrying Eric wipes his forehead.

>   ERIC
>   What are you doing baby?

Pressing several buttons on the keypad on his phone. Getting
frustrated and angry Victoria is unable to unlock the phone.

                          VICTORIA
                    What is the code?

Standing up Eric speaks in aggressive tone.

                          ERIC
                    (Aggressive Tone)
                    You don't need the code. That phone
                    in your hand is mine. I pay that
                    bill not you.

Snatching the phone from Victoria very aggressively Eric
looks and stares at her.

                          ERIC
                    Give me my phone.

Sitting down on the sofa Eric looks at Victoria and smiles.
She reaches and try to grab Eric's phone.

                          VICTORIA
                    Give me this phone.

Laying on top of him they begin to wrestle each other over
the phone.

                          ERIC
                    If you don't get off me.

Eric pushes Victoria off of him. Falling to the floor
shocked from Eric's push Victoria jumps on top of Eric.
Swinging her arms hitting his face and screaming.

                          VICTORIA
                    (Screaming)
                    You motha fucka!

Guarding and protecting his face from being hit Eric
covers it with his hands and arms.

                          ERIC
                    Stop, stop, stop, stop.

Balling his fist he punches Victoria knocking her out to the
floor.

                          ERIC
                    I told you to stop.

As Victoria falls to the floor from the impact of Eric's
punch. Proudly sitting on the sofa Eric watches Victoria
fall and lay on the floor.

EXT./INT. JANICE'S APARTMENT - DAY - AFTERNOON

Victoria rings and knocks on Janice apartment door. Janice opens the door.

                    JANICE
            What's going on sis?

She looks at Janice crying through dark tinted sunglasses.

                    VICTORIA
            A lot can I come in?

Placing her arm around Victoria for comfort Janice escorts her inside the apartment.

                    JANICE
            Of course, come in, come in.

Walking into the apartment Janice looks at Victoria with sympathy. She closes the door and sighs.

INT. JANICE'S APARTMENT - LIVING ROOM - DAY - AFTERNOON

Shutting the door completely Janice looks at Victoria.

                    JANICE
            Vicki, what's wrong?

Victoria walks in Janice's living room crying.

                    VICTORIA
                (Crying)
            A lot.

Sitting on the sofa Victoria cries repeatedly with her head down. Janice walks in the living room and sit next to Victoria.

                    JANICE
            You already said that sis.

Removing the sunglasses off her face slowly raising her head Victoria looks at Janice with watery eyes. Seeing Victoria's eye swollen and bruise Janice gasp and cries.

                    JANICE
                (Gasp and Cry)
            Vicki what happen?

With tears falling down her eyes Victoria looks at Janice.

                                        (CONTINUED)

                              VICTORIA
                         Eric.

Instantly Janice stops crying and becomes very angry.

                              JANICE
                    Eric did this to you?

Victoria nods her head yes. Standing up in front of the sofa
Janice pace back and forth.

                              JANICE
                    I can't believe, he did that.

She stops pacing, turns, and looks at Victoria, then turns
her head to the wall.

                              JANICE
                         Wait, yes I can.

Janice sits back down on the sofa next to Victoria.

                              JANICE
                         What happen?

Looking at Janice crying she make body gestures with her
arms and hands telling the story.

                              VICTORIA
                         (Crying)
                    Eric and I got into a big argument
                    the other night. He got an
                    suspicious phone call when we got
                    home from having dinner at Rose'.

Getting happy and excited listening to Victoria's story
about the restaurant called Rose' Janice smiles.

                              JANICE
                    Ooh, I always want to go there, how
                    is it?

Taking her hand wiping a tear Victoria stops crying and
stares deep into Janice's eyes with anger. Seeing Victoria's
reaction Janice becomes afraid.

                              JANICE
                    Oh, my bad continue.

After hearing Janice's apology Victoria calms down.

                                                    (CONTINUED)

                              VICTORIA
                    So, he gets a phone call then out
                    of nowhere he runs into the
                    bathroom. I chased him down,
                    knocking on the door over and over
                    for like five minutes. He quickly
                    opens the door like nothing happen.

Mouth open from listening to Victoria's story Janice is
shock.

                              JANICE
                    Then what happen?

A little frustrated from Janice's interruptions Victoria
gives her an angry stare.

                              VICTORIA
                    He runs into living room then sits
                    on the sofa and I ask to see his
                    phone. After he takes the phone out
                    of his pocket, he then tries to
                    either delete the number or put
                    some lock code in his phone. I
                    grabbed it then he stands up and
                    gave me a look I never ever seen
                    before and it frightened me. He
                    snatched it back then I jumped on
                    him trying to get the phone back he
                    pushed me off him and then I just
                    snapped. I charged at him and I was
                    just swinging on him, and swinging
                    on him. All I saw was red every
                    time he disrespected me, the
                    cheating, just how he been treating
                    me over the years and all I do is
                    love him. As I'm swinging on him
                    out of nowhere I see his fist
                    coming towards me. Next thing I
                    knew I was alone in bed with an ice
                    pack on my eye.

Becoming angry and upset after hearing Victoria's story
Janice speaks in a angry tone.

                              JANICE
                           (Angry Tone)
                    You need to leave him. Let's go get
                    your things bring them back here
                    and be done with that F.B.

Confuse by Janice comment Victoria side eyes her.

                              VICTORIA
             F.B

Janice smiles and laughs looking at Victoria.

                              JANICE
                         (Laughs)
                    Yeah, fuck boy.

They both laugh at the same time.

                              VICTORIA
                    Easier said than done.

Instantly they stop laughing.

                              JANICE
                    You mean after all this you still
                    want to be with him?

Seriously looking at Janice, wiping a tear from her eye
Victoria sighs.

                              VICTORIA
                         (Sighs)
                    Honestly I don't know what I want
                    to do. I know I love him.

Exhaling Janice place her hand on Victoria's shoulder giving
her a sense of comfort.

                              JANICE
                         (Exhales)
                    Sis, what's love got to do with it?
                    This man put his hands on you
                    that's an ultimate deal breaker. If
                    you let this slide he might kill
                    you next. Knowing he's doing you
                    wrong. You know what, I'm going to
                    call the cops.

She gets off the sofa and walk towards her phone. Victoria
follows her and stops her.

                              VICTORIA
                    No please don't call the cops. I
                    love him.

Suddenly Janice stops her movements as Victoria blocks her
away from the phone.

                              JANICE
                    Well you need to do something, and
                    being a fool is not one of them.

Standing with arms by her sides she looks into Janice eyes.

                              VICTORIA
                    You're right I'm going to get my
                    things and leave him. I can't live
                    the rest of my life like this.
                    Wondering and being afraid of
                    losing him, because I already did.

Thinking about her failed relationship she starts to cry.
Watching her break down and cry Janice walks to and hugs
Victoria.

                              JANICE
                    I'm here for you sis. You know I
                    got you. Everything is going to be
                    alright.

They both close their eyes with a tear from each eye falling
down.

INT. VICTORIA AND ERIC'S APARTMENT - DAY - EVENING

Victoria walks into the apartment. Eric is sitting on the
sofa watching television.

                              ERIC
                    Where have you been all day?

She ignores Eric and walks to the bedroom. He follows her to
the bedroom.

                              ERIC
                    I know you hear me talking to you.

INT. VICTORIA AND ERIC'S APARTMENT - BEDROOM - DAY - EVENING

Walking into the bedroom she grabs luggage bags and proceeds
to put ladies under garments and clothing inside of them.
Shock walking into the bedroom Eric watches Victoria walk
back and forth grabbing her luggage bags and clothes.

                              ERIC
                    What are you doing?

She continues to ignore Eric.

                              ERIC
                    If it's about the other night I
                    apologize, but remember you hit me
                    first.

Packing her belongings she continues to ignore him.

                              ERIC
                    So you're going to leave me? And go
                    where? To Janice's?

Becoming angry with Victoria's actions he approaches
Victoria grabbing her bags and clothes out of her hands.

                              ERIC
                    Bitch, you're not going anywhere.
                    You're my woman and this is your
                    home. Stop this shit.

She removes her hands off the bags.

                            VICTORIA
                    What did you just call me?

Eric throws her bags and clothes on the floor while staring
at Victoria.

                              ERIC
                    Oh, so your speaking to me now.

Folding her arms staring at Eric in a soft aggressive tone
Victoria speaks.

                            VICTORIA
                    You got my attention. So, what did
                    you just call me?

He walks towards Victoria attempting to grab and hold her
hand.

                              ERIC
                    Awww...babe.

Victoria moves her hand and body away from Eric.

                            VICTORIA
                    That's not what you just called me
                    earlier. I'll give you a hint it is
                    a b word.

Unfolding her arms, placing them by her side, Victoria
becomes angry with Eric.

                                              (CONTINUED)

                                    VICTORIA
                          Now, once again, what did you just
                          call me?

Moving his head left to right Eric starts to become
aggravated with Victoria and her questions.

                                    ERIC
                          Here we go with this shit, if you
                          want to leave just leave.

Eric grab one of her belongings and throws it at Victoria.
He walks out the bedroom and into the kitchen. Victoria
follows Eric.

INT. VICTORIA AND ERIC'S APARTMENT - KITCHEN - DAY - EVENING

They both walks into the kitchen, Eric approaches the
refrigerator.

                                    VICTORIA
                          You want me to leave, so you can
                          fuck all them dirty hoes.

Eric opens the refrigerator and grabs a beverage.

                                    ERIC
                          What hoes?

He closes the refrigerator sips his beverage then looks at
Victoria.

                                    VICTORIA
                          I know you've been cheating on me I
                          seen the message in your phone from
                          that hoe weeks ago.

Dropping the beverage on the floor he rushes Victoria
against the wall with his hand wrap around her throat.

                                    ERIC
                          Bitch! You went through my phone?

His eyes is full with rage as he applies pressure to
Victoria's throat choking her to death.

                                    VICTORIA
                                (Choking)
                          I knew that's what you said.

Victoria kicks him in the groin area. Falling back from the
impact of the kick he covers the wounded area with his hand.

She sees a Chef's knife on the kitchen counter. Walking
toward the knife, she grabs the knife off the kitchen
counter. Standing on his feet screaming and yelling Eric
charges at Victoria.

                    ERIC
               (Yells)
          Ahhhh!

Holding the knife to her chest to protect herself from Eric
charging she points it towards him. Running into the knife
Eric falls back with the knife in his chest. While Eric is
laying on the ground Victoria kneels next to him and grabs
the knife stabbing him repeatedly. Screaming and yelling
with blood all over her hands and clothes. Eric's cell phone
begins to ring hearing the last ring she stops stabbing
Eric, putting the knife back in his chest. Victoria goes
into Eric's pocket to get his phone. She looks at Eric phone
and sees a message notification icon. Pressing the
notification button she see a message from a woman with an
provocative picture and a eggplant emoji at the end of her
sentence. Looking away from the phone Victoria stares at
Eric with anger.

                                        INSERT SHOT

                    MESSAGE FROM WOMAN
          Hey baby can't wait to see you I
          miss you and I can't wait to taste
          and lick that sexy ass big ass
          eggplant.

Crying immediately thinking about what she just read and
their entire relationship, staring at Eric's face as the
tears fall down her's. Her eyes move from his face to the
lower region of his body. Taking the knife out of his chest
Victoria screams stabbing directly down Eric's genitals.

                    VICTORIA
               (Screams)
          Ahhhh!

                                        FADE TO BLACK

EXT./INT. JANICE'S APARTMENT - NIGHT - MIDNIGHT

Victoria is standing at the door with her luggage in her
hand in the rain. Janice opens the door.

                    JANICE
          What took so long?

                                        (CONTINUED)

In the doorway standing with dried up blood on her face and
hands with her head down Victoria remain silent. She walks
inside the apartment, Janice stands holding the door
watching her walk inside.

>   JANICE
>   Girl! What happen?

Closing the door

INT. JANICE'S APARTMENT - NIGHT - MIDNIGHT

Standing in front of the door Janice looks at Victoria.

>   JANICE
>   Why do you look like you've been
>   fighting a pack of wolves?

Victoria places her luggage on the floor.

>   VICTORIA
>   It's a long story. I just need a
>   shower right now.

Watching Victoria, looking down at her luggage, slowly
looking up Janice points down a hallway.

>   JANICE
>   You know where to find it.

Quickly grabbing her luggage off the floor Victoria walks
down the hallway.

>   VICTORIA
>   Okay.

With a weird and strange look on her face Janice watches
Victoria walk down the hallway.

INT. JANICE'S APARTMENT - BEDROOM - NIGHT - MIDNIGHT

Janice walks in the bedroom while Victoria is in the
bathroom. Seeing Victoria's luggage she goes through her
belongings, finding a knife with dried blood on it.
Instantly she becomes frighten on what she has discovered.
Looking more into the luggage she sees a man's genitals.
Jumping in fear Janice pushes away the luggage bag. Standing
in the bedroom doorway with a towel wrap around her body
Victoria silently watches.

(CONTINUED)

                        VICTORIA
              What are you doing?

With fear in her eyes Janice looks at Victoria.

                        JANICE
              Nothing.

Victoria walks towards Janice and the luggage bag.

                        VICTORIA
              If you must know, I killed him.

Terrified of what Victoria has revealed, Janice moves away
from the luggage.

                        JANICE
              What do you mean, you killed him?

Grabbing her luggage bag, Victoria opens it, looks inside,
and sees a shirt, and a pair of pants.

                        VICTORIA
              I'm pretty sure you just seen a
              knife in my bag. So you know what I
              mean.

In a hurry grabbing the pair of clothing out of her bag
Victoria begins to pace.

                        VICTORIA
              I got to get out of town.

Janice panics grabbing both Victoria's hands slowing her
down from moving so fast.

                        JANICE
              Wait, what happen?

Stopping her movements she looks at Janice in a calm way.

                        VICTORIA
              Okay, after I left, I went to the
              apartment to get my things liked we
              discussed. While I was packing my
              clothes he was yelling at me asking
              me questions about where have I
              been? Why I'm not talking to him?
              All types of disrespectful shit.
              Then he called me a bitch...

Listening to Victoria's story made Janice very angry.

                                        (CONTINUED)

                              JANICE
                    He called you a what?

Continuing her story slowly calms Janice's anger down.

                              VICTORIA
                    That's what I said and that's what
                    I kept asking him over and over
                    again. He wouldn't repeat it until
                    I told him about me going through
                    his phone and calling him out for
                    cheating on me. He got so mad that
                    I went through his phone without
                    him knowing, he through me against
                    the wall in the kitchen and began
                    to choke me. I was bitch this and
                    bitch that, I got tired of the
                    disrespect. I kicked him in the one
                    that blink not the one that stink.
                    He falls to the ground I was so
                    scared I reached and grabbed the
                    knife off the kitchen counter, he
                    charged at me and I stabbed him.

Shock by Victoria's story Janice completely calms down.

                              JANICE
                    That sounds like to me that was
                    self-defense.

Aggressively grabbing Janice's shoulders becoming frustrated
listening to her comments Victoria speaks passionately.

                              VICTORIA
                    You don't get it Janice. I wanted
                    to kill him. Once he called me out
                    my name, something in me
                    just...just..

Victoria grabs the shirt and pair of pants moving at a fast
pace

                              VICTORIA
                    I got to get out of here.

She takes the clothing and begins to get dress. Janice
calmly speaks to Victoria while watching her get dress.

                              JANICE
                    Where are you going to go?

While finishing getting dress Victoria shrugs her shoulders.

                                                    (CONTINUED)

                         VICTORIA
          I don't know.

She sees a pair of open toe sandals in her luggage bag and
grabs them. Putting on her foot wear Victoria begins to cry.

                         VICTORIA   '
          I don't know what I'm going to do.

Getting closer to Victoria wrapping her arms around her
body, Janice holds and hugs Victoria calming her down.

                         JANICE
          Don't worry I got your back.

Hugging Janice slowly wiping her tears Victoria stops crying
gradually. Extending her arms out with her hands on
Victoria's shoulders Janice stares into her eyes.

                         JANICE
          We need to get you a whole new
          identity. I know somebody that does
          passports IDs whatever you need
          they can do it. I'll just call them
          right now.

Turning away from Victoria walking to look for her phone in
the bedroom. Reaching out placing her hand on Janice's
shoulder Victoria stops her movement.

                         VICTORIA
          Wait, a minute change my identity
          this is happening way to fast.

Removing her hand off Janice's shoulder Victoria walks to
and sits on the bed. Janice walks and sits next to her.

                         JANICE
          You murdered your boyfriend, you
          got to do something and do it fast.
          Before the boys in blue come
          knocking on this door.

Once Janice sits next to her instantly Victoria stands up
and starts pacing back and forth.

                         VICTORIA
          You mention self-defense.

Sitting on the bed Janice watches her pace back and forth.

                         JANICE
                   Sure, can you prove it?

Suddenly Victoria stops pacing and looks at Janice with a
sense of worry.

                         VICTORIA
                   Fuck! I'm screwed.

Attempting to calm her down Janice stands next to Victoria
and pats her back.

                         JANICE
                   Let me just call the guy and get
                   you out of town.

She wraps her arms around Victoria's shoulders giving her a
hug.

                         JANICE
                   I got your back, don't worry about
                   nothing.

Closing her eyes Victoria exhales and smiles.

                         VICTORIA
                      (Exhales, Smiles)
                   Thank you sis.

Pushing away separating from each other Janice stops hugging
Victoria. Glancing at her luggage bag, Janice turns and
looks at her.

                         JANICE
                   Okay, now tell me, why do you have
                   his dick in your bag?

Victoria shrugs her shoulders while looking at Janice.

INT. (FLASHFOWARD) - SIX MONTHS - HOOTERS - DAY - AFTERNOON

Wiping, cleaning off tables, Victoria grabs a tray putting
dirty plates and cups inside of it from each dining table.
Disguised with a dark black wig on her head and eye glasses
on her face.

                         VICTORIA (V.O)
                   Well, Janice friend came through, I
                   change my name to Angela Smith ran
                   away from all my friends and family
                   and ended up in Florida.

                                                    (CONTINUED)

                         DETECTIVE JONES (V.O)
              Florida?

                         VICTORIA (V.O)
              Florida is where I was reborn.

INT. HOOTERS - KITCHEN - DAY - AFTERNOON

A man in his mid 40s walks in the kitchen with an apron on.
Victoria is putting dirty plates and forks into the dish
washer.

                         JACK
              Hey, Angela good work today.

She turns and grab another stack of dirty plates and forks.

                         VICTORIA
              Thanks Jack.

The man leaves the kitchen and walks to the grill. A woman
in her mid 20s walks in the kitchen and places more dirty
dishes on to the counter. She starts to help Victoria put
away the dishes into the dishwasher.

                         KRYSTAL
              Hey, Angela what are you doing
              after work?

Grabbing more stacks of dirty dishes Victoria puts them in
the dishwasher.

                         VICTORIA
              Just lay down, read a good book,
              and be here tomorrow morning.

Krystal stops helping Victoria putting away the dirty
dishes. She leans on the counter and looks at her.

                         KRYSTAL
              You should come out with me and the
              rest of the girls. We're going to
              club Jam Jam tonight.

Stopping her movements taking a short break Victoria stands
at the sink. Victoria turns and look at Krystal.

                         VICTORIA
              No, I'm not the club type.

Getting closer to Victoria persuading her in a creative way
Krystal convinces her to go.

                        KRYSTAL
              Come on girl, come hang out with
              us.

She chuckle and smile looking at Krystal.

                        VICTORIA
              Let me think about it.

Taking a pad and pen off her apron Krystal opens the note
pad walking to the counter. Placing the pad on the counter
Krystal uses the pen as a writing utensil.

                        KRYSTAL
              Okay cool here is my number, if you
              want to link up call me.

While removing the note pad off the counter She rips a piece
of paper off the pad and hands it to Victoria. Victoria
takes the piece of paper and reads it.

                        VICTORIA
              Okay.

Putting the pad and pen back in her apron Krystal smiles.

                        KRYSTAL
                   (Smiles)
              Okay.

She turns and walks out of the kitchen. Placing the paper in
her pocket Victoria turns and continues to place the dirty
dishes in the dishwasher.

INT. NIGHTCLUB JAM JAM - NIGHT - MIDNIGHT

Music: Nightclub Style

Dressed very conservative with an Overcoat Victoria walks
into a nightclub surrounded with a crowd of people at the
bar and on the dance floor. She walks through the crowd then
sees Krystal and three other women in their mid 20s dressed
Raunchy at a private sectional dancing and drinking.

                        KRYSTAL
              Angela over here.

Walking to the table Victoria approaches the four women in
the private sectional.

                         VICTORIA
                    Hey everybody!

Krystal and the three women are dancing, drinking alcohol
beverages and taking pictures in the sectional with their
cell phones.

                       ALL THE WOMEN
                    Hey Angela.

Victoria walks to the table and stands next to Krystal. She
places her Overcoat on the chair behind Krystal. The music
that the DJ is playing throughout the club and the crowd on
the dance floor is so loud, making it hard for people to
communicate. Leaning into Victoria's ear so she will be able
to hear, Krystal yells and ask.

                         KRYSTAL
                    (Yells)
                    What are you drinking?

Slowly Victoria leans into Krystal's ear so she will be able
to hear her answer.

                         VICTORIA
                    Vodka and orange juice.

Shock by Victoria's answer Krystal looks at her and smiles.

                         KRYSTAL
                    Okay girl.

Flagging down a woman in her early 20s with her right hand
Krystal stands and smiles. The waitress walks through the
crowd towards their table. She approaches the table looking
at all five of the women.

                         WAITRESS
                    Hello ladies, how may I help you?

Dancing to the music Krystal stares at the waitress telling
her drink order.

                         KRYSTAL
                    A orange and Vodka for her and a
                    Henny and coke for me.

Turning to look at the other three women dancing with drinks
in their hands Krystal nods.

                         KRYSTAL
                    Y'all good.

Raising their drinks the three women shouts.

                                          (CONTINUED)

                         THREE WOMEN
          Yeah!

She quickly turns back to the waitress to finish her order.

                         KRYSTAL
               Just those two drinks.

Writing down the drink order the waitress looks and smiles.

                         WAITRESS
               Okay, I'll be right back with those
               drinks.

With a smile on her face the waitress walks away from the
table. Listening and dancing to the music (Nightclub Music)
Victoria leans over to Krystal's ear.

                         VICTORIA
               Thanks for the invite.

As the music gets faster and louder Krystal becomes more
excited dancing to the speed of the music.

                         KRYSTAL
               No problem, how you like it so far?

Watching Krystal dance Victoria turns and looks around
observing the nightclub.

                         VICTORIA
               It seems to be an okay place.

Victoria turns to look at Krystal with a surprise and
confuse look on her face.

                         VICTORIA
               So, what made you ask me out?

Walking back to the table with a tray in her right hand with
two glasses of mixed drinks on it the waitress looks and
smiles.

                         WAITRESS
               Here you go ladies.

She places the two drinks down on the table very gently.
Krystal takes out her card and hands it to the waitress.

                         WAITRESS
               I'll be right back with your
               receipt.

                                                    (CONTINUED)

The waitress walks away from the table with Krystal's credit
card in her hand. She grabs her drink and sips it then looks
at Victoria.

                    KRYSTAL
          I don't know you look like you can
          use a friend. You got that I been
          through some shit face so I thought
          maybe this will relax your mind.

Grabbing the orange and Vodka drink Krystal moves it
directly to Victoria. Victoria reaches out and grabs the
drink then sips it.

                    VICTORIA
          Thank you.

Returning back to table with receipt and card in hand, the
waitress hands the receipt, card, and a pen to Krystal.
Taking the pen Krystal signs the receipt.

                    KRYSTAL
          Anytime.

She hands the waitress back her pen and signed receipt.

                    WAITRESS
          An here is your copy. You ladies
          have a good night.

The waitress hands Krystal a copy of the receipt and leaves.
Victoria and Krystal looks at each other toast their
glasses, raise their drinks, sip them, then screams to the
music.

INT. HOOTERS - KITCHEN - NIGHT - EVENING

Victoria is in the kitchen cleaning and prepping for the
morning shift. A man in his mid 40s walks in the kitchen
watching Victoria in a inappropriate way.

                    JACK
          Hey Angela good job today.

Smiling while cleaning and prepping Victoria looks and sees
Jack standing by the kitchen entrance and exit doors.

                    VICTORIA
          Hey Jack, thank you. I like to
          work.

Jack stares at Victoria with lustful eyes. He looks at
Victoria's feet up to her thighs to her chest. Looking at
Victoria's smile, eyes, and body Jack begins to grin.

                    MANAGER
          Jack get back on this grill I need
          some wings and a burger cook.

Standing by the exit doors Jack stares and smiles.

                    JACK
          Coming, excuse me Angela.

Leaving the kitchen Jack walks through the exit door.

INT. VICTORIA'S APARTMENT - KITCHEN - NIGHT - MIDNIGHT

In the kitchen putting dirty dishes in the sink Victoria
prepares to wash them. She hears a knock on the door.
Turning the faucet off Victoria leaves the kitchen and
begins to walk towards the front door.

INT. VICTORIA'S APARTMENT - HALLWAY - FRONT DOOR - NIGHT -
MIDNIGHT

Victoria walks to the front door, looks through the peek
hole seeing Jack standing in front of the door.

                    VICTORIA
          Who is it?

Jack is standing in front of the door with a smile on his
face.

                    JACK
          It's Jack.

Looking through the peek hole Victoria is shock and frighten
by the surprise visit from Jack.

                    VICTORIA
          Jack? How the hell you know where I
          live?

She slowly opens the door.

                    VICTORIA
          What are you doing here?

He stands in the door way with a huge smile on his face.

                                                    (CONTINUED)

                         JACK
               Angela! You live here? What a
               coincidence!

Rolling her eyes listening to Jack's excuse Victoria smirks.

                         JACK
               My car broke down in front of the
               apartment building and my phone is
               dead. Can I use your phone to call
               triple A?

Opening the door wide enough for Jack to walk in Victoria
shrugs her shoulders.

                         VICTORIA
               Sure.

Walking into the apartment Jack giggles as Victoria closes
the door.

                         VICTORIA
               Wait right here, I got to get my
               phone.

She walks down the hallway into her bedroom. Jack locks the
door then follows Victoria quietly.

                         JACK
               Thank you for your help Angela.

INT. VICTORIA'S APARTMENT - BEDROOM - NIGHT - MIDNIGHT

Victoria walks in the bed room to her nightstand grabs her
phone then suddenly turns and sees Jack.

                         VICTORIA
               I told you to wait...what are you
               doing in here? Here's the phone get
               out.

Handing him the phone Victoria pushes Jack out of the room.
He grabs the phone from her hand walking slowly out of the
bed room. After dialing a mixture of numbers on the phone he
puts the phone to his ear.

                         JACK
               Okay, I'm going. Hi I'm Jack
               Roberts and I need a jump pronto.

INSERT SHOT OF A BLACK SCREEN ON THE PHONE

Nodding his head quickly glancing at Victoria.

                                              (CONTINUED)

                              JACK
               Uhh...huh. Forty-five minutes, okay
               yes I'm somewhere safe. I'm at a
               friend's apartment.

Talking on the phone he looks and smiles at Victoria.

                              JACK
               Yes call me from this number, okay
               I'll be waiting by the phone. Okay,
               thank you for your help. Bye-bye.

Removing the phone from his ear ending the phone call. While
giving back her phone Jack smiles in a flirtatious way.

                              JACK
               Here you go, and thanks again.

Grabbing the phone from Jack's hand Victoria pushes him
completely out of the room.

                              VICTORIA
               No problem. Now get out. Forty-five
               minutes uh?

Jack leaves the room Victoria follows closing the doors.

                              JACK
               Yes ma'am.

INT. VICTORIA'S APARTMENT - HALLWAY - NIGHT - MIDNIGHT

In a awkward silence Victoria and Jack stands in the hallway
looking at each other.

                              VICTORIA
               Since you got to wait, would you
               like something to drink?

Jack smiles moving his head in a up and down motion.

                              JACK
               Sure.

Victoria and Jack walks to the kitchen.

INT. VICTORIA'S APARTMENT - KITCHEN - NIGHT - MIDNIGHT

They walk inside the kitchen.

                    VICTORIA
          I was just washing dishes.

Jack sits by the kitchen table looking at Victoria. Victoria
walks to the refrigerator. She opens the refrigerator bends
over and look inside the refrigerator.

                    VICTORIA
          Would you like some water, juice,
          or soda?

He looks at Victoria's rear-end with a smile on his face
whispering to himself.

                    JACK
          Very nice.

Still looking inside the refrigerator Victoria hears Jack
talking.

                    VICTORIA
          What you say?

Feeling embarrass he quickly responds.

                    JACK
          Water with ice.

Searching inside the refrigerator she looks and sees the
bottle of water in the refrigerator.

                    VICTORIA
          Okay.

Grabbing the bottle of water out of the refrigerator
Victoria closes the refrigerator door. Then she walks to the
kitchen counter near a cabinet. Placing the water bottle on
top of the counter she opens the cabinet door. Cups and
plates are place inside she grabs a cup then closes the
cabinet door. Putting the cup next to the water bottle
Victoria walks to the refrigerator opens the freezer then
grabs the ice tray. She closes the freezer door walks to the
counter with the ice tray in hand. Removing two ice cubes
from the ice tray and placing them in the cup Victoria
turns, look at Jack, and smiles. After putting ice cubes in
the cup Victoria walks back to the refrigerator to put the
ice tray back in the freezer. Closing the freezer she walks
to the counter, grabs the cup with ice, and the water bottle
off the counter. Walking towards Jack she looks and smiles

                                        (CONTINUED)

handing him the cup and bottle of water. He takes the cup
and water bottle from Victoria with a big smile on his face.

                    JACK
          Thank you.

Still smiling Victoria turns and walks away from Jack.

                    VICTORIA
          No problem.

Approaching the kitchen sink Victoria turns it on to warm
water temperature. She takes the dish washing liquid and
sponge/rag and proceed to wash her dirty dishes. While
sipping his drink of water Jack watches Victoria at the
sink. Looking her up and down he whispers to himself.

                    JACK
                (Whispers)
          Very nice.

He place the drink on the kitchen table and stands up.
Slowly he walks behind Victoria, whispers in her ear, while
grinding on her at the same time. Startled by his actions
she pushes Jack onto the kitchen table knocking the cup off
it. Hitting the floor Jack lays on his back.

                    VICTORIA
          Get off me!

Sitting up in rage he touches the back of his head checking
for blood. He looks at Victoria in anger.

                    JACK
                (Angry)
          Fucking crazy bitch.

Standing in front of the sink looking at Jack she becomes
angry.

                    VICTORIA
          What did you just call me?

Getting off the floor he stands up.

                    JACK
          I thought you like me, I like you.
          Hell I thought we could have some
          fun together.

Watching Jack stands up Victoria becomes terrified.

                                              (CONTINUED)

                         VICTORIA
                    So you wanted to rape me?

Shaking his head Jack stands looking at Victoria

                         JACK
                    Rape that's such a strong word.
                    Let's call it a test drive. Now
                    come on you know you want it let me
                    ram this anaconda in you.

Rushing towards Victoria yelling and screaming with
aggression Jack gyrates repeatedly.

                         JACK
                    Ahhh!

She kicks Jack in the groin he falls down to the floor.

                         VICTORIA
                    I told you to get off me.

Rolling back and forth in pain holding his groin Jack
screams.

                         JACK
                       (Screams)
                    Fuck you, you crazy bitch!

Hearing the words that Jack just screamed makes Victoria go
into a rage.

                         VICTORIA
                    What did you just call me?

Placing her hand in the sink feeling the different eating
utensils three forks, two spoons, and one Chef's knife.
Feeling a sharp point on her finger she puts her hand on the
utensil. Recognizing her hand is on the Chef's knife
standing with confidence Victoria stares at Jack with a evil
grin. Jack raise himself up off the floor slowly and stands
up.

                         JACK
                    Crazy...bitch.

Putting her hand around the knife's hand grip she slowly
moves it in the water.

                         VICTORIA   .
                    Thought so.

                                              (CONTINUED)

Raising his arms reaching towards Victoria opening both
hands wrapping them around Victoria's neck/throat. Grabbing
the knife Victoria takes it out of the water and stabs Jack
in his chest. Falling to floor Jack bleeds rapidly. Standing
over his dead bloody body she looks at him with pride.

                    VICTORIA
          You wanted to rape who, who me, you
          picked the wrong one. Bitch!

Victoria laughs looking down, around his male genital area.

                    VICTORIA
               (Laughs)
          You want be needing this anymore.

Directing the knife down to his male genitals she swings it
in a cutting motion.

                                        FADE TO BLACK

EXT./INT. KRYSTAL'S APARTMENT - DAY - MORNING

Krystal hears a knock on her front door. She opens the door
and sees Victoria standing in the shadows.

                    VICTORIA
          Do you remember, when you told me
          about me needing a friend?

Seeing Victoria in the shadows nervously Krystal responds.
Getting a small glimpse of Victoria in the light she sees
her wearing dark sweat pants and a old dingy dirty T-shirt.

                    KRYSTAL
          Yeah.

Victoria steps into the light.

                    VICTORIA
          You were right. I need a friend,
          like right now.

Skeptical of the situation she quickly hurries Victoria into
her apartment.

                    KRYSTAL
          Come in.

Walking into the apartment Victoria is grateful for
Krystal's hospitality.

>   VICTORIA
>   Thank you.

Stepping outside of her apartment Krystal looks around her
front door with a sense of suspicion.

>   KRYSTAL
>   No problem.

She sees a car that looks very familiar to her (Jack's car).

>   KRYSTAL
>   Angela, who car is that?

Closing the front door Krystal walks inside the apartment.

INT. KRYSTAL'S APARTMENT - DAY - MORNING

Victoria looks around Krystal's apartment admiring it.

>   VICTORIA
>   Very nice. You got good taste.

Worrying about the way Victoria appeared at her home Krystal
has a concern look on her face.

>   KRYSTAL
>   Thank you. When you called, you
>   said, "it was urgent." What's
>   wrong?

Calmly Victoria looks at Krystal and reveals the car keys
out of her pocket.

>   VICTORIA
>   The car I need to leave it with
>   you, I got to leave town.

Still confuse Krystal questions Victoria's actions.

>   KRYSTAL
>   Why do you need to leave town? What
>   do you want me to do with the car?

Placing her hand on Krystal's shoulder Victoria looks and
winks at her.

>   VICTORIA
>   Keep it, I got to go.

Rushing to the door Victoria removes her hand off Krystal's
shoulder. Krystal steps into Victoria's path blocking the
door way.

                                        (CONTINUED)

                              KRYSTAL
                  Wait, what is going on?

She gives Krystal a quick glance and smirks.

                              VICTORIA
                         (Smirks)
                  I'm leaving town, that's all you
                  need to know. Oh and You're going
                  to need to get new plates for it.

Victoria hands Krystal the car keys then walks pass her to
the front door. Opening the door she exits, with the car
keys in her hand standing confuse Krystal watches Victoria
walk out the front door.

                              KRYSTAL
                  What?

EXT. KRYSTAL'S APARTMENT - DAY - MORNING

Victoria is walking away from Krystal's apartment. She grabs
her phone out of her pocket. Holding her phone she presses a
mixture of numeric buttons then place the phone to her ear.

                              VICTORIA
                  Hey, this Vicki I need another
                  favor.

INT. HOTEL - HOTEL ROOM - NIGHT - EVENING

Victoria is sitting on the hotel bed in the dark crying
thinking about the bad things she has done.

INSERT SHOT FLASHBACK OF HER MURDERING THE TWO MEN

Developing a evil grin on her face while reminiscing she
stands and walks to the hotel mirror.

                              VICTORIA
                  They will all pay, all abusive and
                  evil men must die!

Holding a knife in her hand she looks at the mirror staring
at her reflection. Hearing a ghostly whisper in her head she
sees her evil half/twin self appearing in the mirror.

                              VICTORIA EVIL SIDE
                  I want to come out and play. I've
                  developed a thirst I don't think we
                  should stop.

                                                    (CONTINUED)

Looking at her evil side in the mirror she accept her evil
self, turning, and becoming evil completely.

                    VICTORIA
          And I won't stop.

INT. LORENZO'S BAR & GRILL - NIGHT - MIDNIGHT

Two men sitting at a bar in their late 30s next to a woman
in her mid 20s harassing her with name calling. Victoria is
sitting far away at a table in the shadows. She disguise
herself with a long dark wig and a seductive dress. Watching
the two men and the woman at the bar she slowly sips her
drink. One of the men whisper in the other man's ear while
they look at the woman at the bar. The woman jump up out of
her chair and start to yell at one of the men for placing
his hand on her leg. Observing everything from her table in
the shadows she sips her drink and quickly exits the bar.
Open hand slapping the man making everyone in the bar stop
their movements watching the woman stare down the man.
Instantly the man gets angry at the woman. He charges at the
woman the Bartender steps in front of him preventing the
woman from getting hurt. Protecting the woman the Bartender
signals the Security men in the club to take both of the men
out of the bar. Two Security men grab the two men and toss
them out the bar through the front door.

EXT. LORENZO'S BAR & GRILL - NIGHT - MIDNIGHT

Victoria watches the two men being toss out the club from
across the street in the shadows. The two men gets off the
ground and walks towards their car. One standing next to the
driver side door and the other standing next to the
passenger side door. Opening the car doors, stepping inside,
and closing the car doors the two men sits inside angry. She
walks in front of the car slow and seductively. Stopping
their movements in the car the men stares at Victoria with
lustful eyes. Standing in front of the car she stops, turns,
and looks at the two men.

                    VICTORIA
          Can you boys give me a ride home?

Sitting in the car staring at Victoria the two men becomes
excited.

                    MEN
          Hell yeah! Come on in.

Victoria walks to the car opens the backseat door and steps
inside then closes the door.

                                              (CONTINUED)

                              VICTORIA
                    Thanks fellas.

Man 1 is sitting in the passenger seat with a huge smile on
his face. He turns and look at Victoria with excitement.

                              MAN 1
                    No problem, a gorgeous woman like
                    yourself should not be alone and
                    walking around at this time of
                    night. They're all types of
                    crazyeees and crazzooos.

She looks at Man 1 and nods her head.

                              VICTORIA
                    I agree.

Man 2 starts the car and drives off.

INT. THE TWO MEN'S APARTMENT - DAY - MORNING

Male and female Detectives, Police Patrolmen, and CSI (Crime
Scene Investigator) Agents are walking around the apartment
taking pictures, asking questions, and taking notes. The two
men from the bar are laying on the floor naked with knife
cuts and markings all over their bodies. Lying on the floor
with blood all over them and their male genitals remove,
shocks everyone in the apartment. Detective Jones arrives to
the crime scene walking over the caution tape and towards a
CSI Agent. Speaking to a CSI Agent male in their mid 30s
Detective Jones looks at the victims and around the
apartment.

                              DETECTIVE JONES
                    What do we got?

CSI Agent 1 is examining the two male bodies with latex
gloves on his hands. He shows Detective Jones the knife cuts
that are on the victims.

                              CSI AGENT 1
                    Two males slit from the neck down
                    to their chest. And they both been
                    Lorena Bobbitt.

With a look of pain Detective Jones looks at the CSI Agent
and ask.

                              DETECTIVE JONES
                    You mean?

Pointing at the victims genital area the CSI Agent looks at
Detective Jones.

                         CSI AGENT 1
               Yes sir.

They both grab their groins at the same time. Removing his
hand from his groin Detective Jones looks at CSI Agent 1.

                         DETECTIVE JONES
               Murder weapon?

Looking at Detective Jones removing his hand from his groin
CSI Agent 1 moves his head from left to right.

                         CSI AGENT 1
               No sir. This killer is smart no
               finger prints no force entry.

Detective Jones look the victims up and down looking at
their wounds.

                         DETECTIVE JONES
               No force entry, that means it's
               probably someone they know?

CSI Agent 1 looks at his notepad and writes down notes.

                         CSI AGENT 1
               Most likely.

Grabbing a pair of latex gloves from one of the CSI Agents
in the apartment. Examining and walking around the apartment
Detective Jones looks for any type of clues.

                         CSI AGENT 1
               Do you see anything sir.

Noticing plates and cups on a table. He takes a black light
out of his pocket, picks up one of the plates, and examines
it. Seeing no result he puts it down back on the table.
Repeating the process with the black light he examine one of
the cups on the table and sees no results. Placing the cup
back on the table Detective Jones becomes disappointed.

                         DETECTIVE JONES
               Nope, nothing.

INT. POLICE PRECINCT - DAY - EVENING

Detective Jones is sitting at his desk going through photos
and notes from the crime scene. The Captain of the precinct
in his late 50s steps out of his office and yells.

                    CAPTAIN PITTS
               (Yells)
          Jones!

Standing up out of his desk chair Detective Jones looks and
sees Captain Pitts.

                    DETECTIVE JONES
          Sir.

Captain Pitts looks at Detective Jones and shouts.

                    CAPTAIN PITTS
               (Shouts)
          Get in here!

He walks to and inside Captain Pitts office. After Detective
Jones walks in the office Captain Pitts closes his office
door.

INT. POLICE PRECINCT - CAPTAIN PITTS OFFICE - DAY - EVENING

Detective sees an athletic built male in his late 30s early
40s sitting in a chair across from Captain Pitts desk.
Standing by the door next to Captain Pitts.

                    CAPTAIN PITTS
          This is Agent Chase he's from the
          FBI.

Captain Pitts points at the athletic male sitting in a chair
across from his desk.

                    CAPTAIN PITTS
          He has an interest in your case.

He walks to his desk and sits in the chair. Agent Chase
stands, turns, and looks at Detective Jones.

                    AGENT CHASE
          Yeah, I'm intrigued how your
          victims have been attacked. It's
          the same as a couple of cold cases
          from two different states. The
          victims names were Eric Fields and
          Jack Foster.

(CONTINUED)

He hands Detective Jones a file containing information on
Eric and Jack. Detective Jones is briefly looking through
the file. Amaze he sees notes of information about the way
the victims were murdered, autopsy photos, and their back
ground information.

                    DETECTIVE JONES
          This is similar.

Pointing at the file, looking at Detective Jones, sitting
back in the chair Agent Chase turns his head towards Captain
Pitts.

                    AGENT CHASE
          These cold cases and your case are
          similar. We got a serial killer on
          our hands and it's thirsty for
          blood.

Seeing Detective Jones standing by the door Captain Pitts
points at him and then points at the chair next to Agent
Chase.

                    CAPTAIN PITTS
          Have a seat.

Sitting next to Agent Chase across from Captain Pitts desk
Detective Jones stares at him in attentive way. Looking at
each other Captain Pitts watches Detective Jones reclines in
the chair.

                    CAPTAIN PITTS
          Since you are the lead Detective on
          this case and the FBI wants to be
          apart of it, I think you two should
          work together on it. So welcome
          Agent Chase with open arms, show
          him the ropes, and bring this
          killer to justice.

Turning his head to Agent Chase slowly moving his head
forward Detective Jones looks at Captain Pitts.

                    DETECTIVE JONES
          Yes sir.

Agent Chase nods his head at Captain Pitts. They both get
out of the chairs, stands up, and leaves Captain Pitts'
office.

INT. SWEET ROSES HOTEL - ROOM 69 - NIGHT - MIDNIGHT

A elderly man in his mid 50 is escorted by Victoria disguise
in a dark wig, red lipstick, stylish heels, and a seductive
dress standing by the hotel room door. With a fashionable
purse around her shoulder Victoria and the man walks in the
room. The man closes the hotel room door.

                    ROBERT
          Oh baby I've been thinking about
          you all day, I couldn't wait to get
          with you.

Robert walks to and sits on the bed. Victoria stands in
front and looks at Robert.

                    VICTORIA
          Robert Jones?

Smiling with excitement Robert tries to put his hands on
Victoria's body.

                    ROBERT
               (Smiles)
          Yes, that's me!

Victoria stares into his eyes placing her hand on his chin
squeezing it aggressively speaking in a tone of anger.

                    VICTORIA
               (Angry tone)
          The same Robert Jones, who beat and
          verbally abuse his wife?

He looks at her very confused placing his hands on the bed.

                    ROBERT
          Wait, what's going on here? I
          thought we came here to...

She grabs a knife out of her purse, he panics with fear.

                    ROBERT
               (Panics)
          Wait...No!

                                        CUT TO BLACK

INT. DETECTIVE JONES APARTMENT - KITCHEN - DAY - MORNING

Standing by the stove and oven Detective Jones grabs a
coffee mug that's on the kitchen counter. Sipping his coffee
watching the news on the television preparing his breakfast
Detective Jones steps closer to the television.

                    ANCHOR MAN
          Breaking news a murder in Atlanta
          Georgia at the Sweet Roses Hotel. A
          fifty-five year old man named
          Robert Jones was slit from his neck
          down to his private area. Which is
          no more, Do we have a Lorena
          Bobbitt copy cat?

Still sipping his coffee Detective Jones chokes and coughs
nearly burning himself. Shock by the news he over cooks
the breakfast destroying it compeletly.

                    ANCHOR MAN
          Police say no evidence, have been
          found.

He turns cooking equipment and television off.

EXT. AIR PORT - DAY - NOON

Agent Chase is walking to a helicopter. Detective Jones
drives up to the helicopter and suddenly stops. He gets out
of his car and yells.

                    DETECTIVE JONES
               (Yells)
          Chase!

Hearing his name being yelled Agent Chase stops walking,
turns his body towards the voice, and see Detective Jones
walking to him. He approaches Agent Chase gasping for air.

                    DETECTIVE JONES
               (Gasping)
          I want to be apart of this case.

Moving his head left to right Agent Chase looks at Detective
Jones very stern.

                    AGENT CHASE
          No, this is way out of your
          jurisdiction.

He stops moving his head looking at Detective Jones.

                                        (CONTINUED)

                         AGENT CHASE
               This damn serial killer has crossed
               multiple state lines. He is now a
               threat to this country. So, don't
               worry we will take care of it.

With a questionable look on his face Detective Jones raises
his eyebrow looking at Agent Chase.

                         DETECTIVE JONES
               How do you know it's a he?

Giggling to Detective Jones question Agent Chase confidently
responds.

                         AGENT CHASE
                         (Giggles)
               No woman is this violent.

Persuading Agent Chase to change his thought Detective Jones
demonstrates with hand movements.

                         DETECTIVE JONES
               Come on the Lorena Bobbitt
               signature.

Impress by Detective Jones with a smile on his face Agent
Chase pats Detective Jones on his shoulder welcoming him to
the helicopter.

                         AGENT CHASE
               You might be right. Come on get in.

They walk to the helicopter, steps inside, sits down in the
passenger seats, then put their seat belts on as the
propellers turn.

                         AGENT CHASE
               Your Captain said, "bring this
               killer to justice" and that's what
               we're going to do.

Agent Chases closes the helicopter door. The helicopter
takes off to the sky.

INT. POLICE PRECINCT - DAY - EVENING

Knocking on the precinct Captain's door Agent Chase stands
in the door way holding his badge at the door. A male in his
mid 50s opens the door. He sees Agent Chase with his FBI
Badge pointed at his face moving his eyes to the right
seeing Detective Jones standing next to him.

                    AGENT CHASE
          Hello sir I'm Agent Chase from the
          FBI and this is my partner, Agent
          Jones.

Putting his badge away Agent Chase points at his self and
Detective Jones to the Captain.

                    CAPTAIN SMITTY
          Come on in fellas.

They walk inside Captain Smitty's office. Captain Smitty
closes the door.

INT. POLICE PRECINCT - CAPTAIN SMITTY'S OFFICE - DAY -
EVENING

Captain Smitty walks to his desk and sits in his chair.

                    CAPTAIN SMITTY
          How may I help you gentlemen?

Detective Jones and Agent Chase each sits in one of the two
chairs across from Captain Smitty.

                    AGENT CHASE
          My partner and I have been trailing
          this Lorena Bobbitt copy cat for
          awhile. Which lead us here. We were
          wondering, if you had any
          information that could help our
          investigation?

Leaning back in his chair Captain Smitty looks at Agent
Chase and Detective Jones.

                    CAPTAIN SMITTY
          Look guys I would love to help, but
          there was nothing at the crime
          scene.

He points at the door with his index finger.

                    CAPTAIN SMITTY
          But you can talk to Jefferson
          that's his case. He's at his desk
          writing his report.

Grateful for Captain Smitty's help Agent Chase looks at him
and smile.

                                        (CONTINUED)

                        AGENT CHASE
              Thank you sir.

Looking at Captain Smitty sitting in the chair Detective
Jones smiles and nods.

                        DETECTIVE JONES
              Thank you sir.

Pulling his hand away from the direction of the door Captain
Smitty stands up and reaches out for a handshake from Agent
Chase and Detective Jones.

                        CAPTAIN SMITTY
              No, problem. Welcome to Atlanta.

Agent Chase and Detective Jones stands up out of the chairs,
shakes Captain Smitty hand, stop shaking his hand, and
leaves the office. Sitting back in his chair Captain Smitty
grabs the phone on his desk.

INT. POLICE PRECINCT - DAY - EVENING

Approaching a desk Agent Chase and Detective Jones both sees
a name plate on top of it. The name plate reads "Michael
Jefferson." Agent Chase reads the plate then looks at a male
in his late 30s early 40s.

                        AGENT CHASE
              Jefferson? Michael Jefferson? Are
              you the same Jefferson that's
              covering the Lorena Bobbitt copy
              cat case?

Typing on his computer Detective Michael Jefferson looks up
and see Agent Chase and Detective Jones.

                        DETECTIVE JEFFERSON
              Whose asking?

Agent Chase shows Detective Jefferson his FBI badge.

                        AGENT CHASE
              I'm Agent chase from the FBI and
              this is my partner Agent Jones.

Detective Jones nods his head looking at Detective
Jefferson, putting away his badge Agent Chase places his
hands on his side.

                                                     (CONTINUED)

                         AGENT CHASE
               We have been on this psycho
               murderous trail for awhile and we
               always hit a dead end. Do you have
               anything that can possibly help our
               investigation.

Quickly placing his hand on the desk drawer handle Detective
Jefferson looks at Agent Chase.

                         DETECTIVE JEFFERSON
               This killer is smart, I looked
               around and dusted everything.
               Nothing, no murder weapon, no DNA
               just a missing penis. I do have the
               surveillance footage of the front
               desk from the hotel.

He open his desk drawer grabs a DVD with a cover over it and
hands it to Agent Chase. Agent Chase looks at the DVD then
looks at Detective Jefferson.

                         AGENT CHASE
               What's on it?

Sitting in his chair Detective Jefferson points at the DVD
that is in Agent Chase's hand.

                         DETECTIVE JEFFERSON
               We got an idea who Robert Jones was
               with that night he was murdered.

Both turning their heads towards each other Agent Chase and
Detective Jones smiles.

INT. ATLANTA GEORGIA - FBI HEADQUARTERS - OFFICE - NIGHT -
EVENING

Detective Jones and Agent Chase are sitting watching the
security/ surveillance footage on a computer monitor. The
footage shows Robert walking to the front desk with a woman
on his arm purchasing a room. Watching the footage Detective
Jones notice a woman next to Robert, but couldn't see her
face.

                         DETECTIVE JONES
               Pause it.

Agent Chase pauses the video, Detective Jones points at the
woman on the monitor.

                                                (CONTINUED)

                          DETECTIVE JONES
                  I told you it was a woman.

Staring at the monitor Agent Chase is shock as he press play
to view the rest of the video.

                          AGENT CHASE
                  Well damn, you were right.

Both stares at the monitor watching the whole security video
of Robert and Victoria walking to and away from the
check-out counter.

                          DETECTIVE JONES
                  Now, What?

Detective Jones turns his head away from the computer
monitor and looks at Agent Chase.

                          AGENT CHASE
                  We wait until she strikes again and
                  hopefully this time we can find out
                  who this woman is.

INSERT SHOT OF WOMAN IN THE SURVEILLANCE TAPE/FOOTAGE

INT. COFFEE SHOP - DAY - AFTERNOON

Victoria is sitting at a table sipping a cup of coffee. She
looks up at the television and sees a man in his mid 40s on
the screen.

                          NEWS ANCHOR
                  Breaking News, the Lorena Bobbitt
                  copy cat strikes again this time
                  the killer has migrated to Alabama.
                  Investigators has discovered that
                  this cold blooded killer is a
                  woman. The woman's identity has not
                  yet been determined.

After placing her cup on the table she puts down the exact
amount of money on the table for the coffee bill. Standing
up out of her seat she looks at the clerk he glance at her.
She winks at him then exits the coffee shop.

EXT. OUTSIDE - CITY PARK - NIGHT - EVENING

Victoria is walking in a city park disguise with a long
black wig with black leather on. She sees two men in their
early 20s and a woman in her late 20s walking in the park.
The men are harassing, catcalling, grabbing, pushing and
yelling at her on the ground.

                    WOMAN
          Stop, get your hands off me.

Swinging her arms hitting the men as they stand over her
tearing the clothing off her body. She yells and screams
repeatedly.

                    WOMAN
               (Screams)
          Help!

The men laugh while grabbing the woman's body parts.

                    MAN 2
          You know you like it, stop fighting
          it.

Man 3 holds her arms down on the ground.

                    MAN 3
          Yeah, all we need is 10 minutes.
          five for me and five for my friend.

Both laughing aggressively touching and kissing on the
woman's face and breast. Victoria approaches the men and the
woman.

                    VICTORIA
          Hey, what don't you guys leave her
          alone?

Stopping their movements the men turns their heads to look
at Victoria. While the men are distracted the woman quickly
gets off the ground and runs away. She looks at the men with
a seductive smile.

                    VICTORIA
          If you want to have a good time all
          you have to do is ask.

Flaunting her breast and rear-end Victoria winks at them in
a very flirtatious way. The two men stands and stares at
Victoria with lustful eyes.

                                            (CONTINUED)

                         VICTORIA
                   So gentlemen, what do you want to
                   do?

They both look at each other and smile.

INT. FBI HEADQUARTERS - CONFERENCE ROOM - DAY - EVENING

Detective Jones is sitting reviewing the case files and
photos at a round table. He stands and places the pictures
on a board with red line markings connecting to each other
creating a investigation board. Staring at the board
Detective Jones becomes dazed. Agent Chase approaches
Detective Jones tapping him on the shoulder which startled
him.

                         AGENT CHASE
                   So...

Walking back and forth from the round table to the
investigation board Detective Jones skims through multiple
page reports and photos of the case. He stops, turns, and
looks at Agent Chase.

                         DETECTIVE JONES
                   There's a connection to her
                   targets.

Turning back to the investigation board Detective Jones
stares and looks at the images on the board.

                         DETECTIVE JONES
                   I just got to figure out, what it
                   is.

Watching Detective Jones look at the board Agent Chase
glances at the board and stares at the images.

                         AGENT CHASE
                   You might want to also check the
                   computer database on these victims.
                   Something about them maybe a
                   trigger for her. For her to react
                   in such a cruel manner towards
                   them.

He exits the room. One step closer to the investigation
board Detective Jones stares at the images on the board.

                         DETECTIVE JONES
                   We know for one thing, all of them
                   are missing their...oh, sh...

INT. VICTORIA'S APARTMENT - DAY - EVENING

Victoria is sitting in a dark room dress in all black. Her collection of the victims' male genitals are displayed all over the apartment. She laughs sadistically over and over again.

EXT. OUTSIDE - DAY - AFTERNOON

Agent Chase is walking and talking on his phone.

>   AGENT CHASE
>   Yeah, still nothing, but Jones has
>   been working hard. All we need for
>   her to do is make one bad slip up.
>   She can't be this perfect,
>   eventually she's going to get cocky
>   and that's when she will make that
>   slip. Don't worry I'm on it.

He hangs up his phone.

INT. FBI HEADQUARTERS - DAY - EVENING

Detective Jones is sitting at a desk in front of the computer. Searching on the criminal computer database he discover criminal information on one of Victoria's victims. Reading the information on the computer it indicates Jack had a domestic abuse and criminal assault charge towards a woman 3 years ago and Robert a year ago. A fellow Agent startled Detective Jones as he's looking at the computer.

>   AGENT 1
>   Jones? You got a phone call.

The Agent exits after telling Detective Jones about the phone call. Detective Jones quickly grabs and answers the phone on the desk.

>   DETECTIVE JONES
>   Jones!

>   INTER CUT

EXT. OUTSIDE - DAY - EVENING

Agent chase has his cell phone to his ear.

(CONTINUED)

                              AGENT CHASE
                    Hey, this is Chase, did you find
                    anything yet?

                                                        INTER CUT

INT. FBI HEADQUARTERS - DAY - EVENING

Sitting at the desk Detective Jones has the phone to his ear
as he's looking at the computer.

                              DETECTIVE JONES
                    Nothing really concrete, but there
                    is this one thing you need to see.
                    It might be something, but then
                    again it might be nothing. It's
                    just a hunch of mine.

Walking down the sidewalk Agent Chase sees a corner store.

                              AGENT CHASE
                    Be there in a moment.

Continuing looking at the computer Detective Jones starts to
remove the phone off his ear.

                              DETECTIVE JONES
                    See you when you get here.

Both Detective Jones and Agent Chase hangs up the phone.

EXT. OUTSIDE - DAY - EVENING

Looking up to the sky Agent Chase closes his eyes.

                              AGENT CHASE
                    Please be something.

INT. STORE MART - DAY - EVENING

A male teenager walks inside the neighborhood/corner store.

CLOSE UP: OF BELL HANGING ON THE DOOR

SFX: Ringing of store bell

Standing in line to purchase and item from the store Agent
Chase looks around the store. He hears a Breaking News
Announcement from the Store Clerk radio behind the counter.

                                                       (CONTINUED)

                         ANCHOR MAN
                    Breaking News the DB slasher aka LB
                    the second, is at it again this
                    time Louisiana. Two male victims,
                    twenty-two year old William Smith
                    and twenty-two year old Phillip
                    Duncan was found at the Sweet Sweet
                    Motel and you guess it both are
                    missing a...

After a patron leaves the line with his/hers items Agent
Chase walks to the counter. The Store Clerk turns off the
radio then looks at Agent Chase.

                         STORE CLERK
                    Five, fifty-five.

Throwing a ten dollar bill on the counter Agent Chase grabs
his purchased items.

                         AGENT CHASE
                    Keep the change.

He rushes and leaves the store in a hurry.

EXT./INT. CAR - SIDEWALK - DAY - EVENING

Detective Jones is standing and waiting on the sidewalk.
Agent Chase drives up to the curb of the sidewalk.

                         AGENT CHASE
                    Get in.

Opening the passenger side car door Detective Jones steps
inside leaving the door open.

                         AGENT CHASE
                    Did you hear?

He turns his head to look at Agent Chase.

                         DETECTIVE JONES
                    Yeah.

They both look at each other.

                         BOTH DETECTIVE JONES AND AGENT CHASE
                    Louisiana!

Closing the passenger side car door Detective Jones puts the
seat belt across him. Sitting in the car Agent Chase watches
Detective Jones close the car door, turning his head to the
road, he then drives off.

EXT./INT. CAR - DAY - EVENING

Agent Chase is driving the car. Detective Jones is sitting
in the passenger seat. Both are in the car with seat belts
wrapped across their bodies.

                    DETECTIVE JONES
          I got a hunch.

Driving down the road Agent Chase quickly glances at
Detective Jones.

                    AGENT CHASE
          What is it?

Detective Jones turns his head to look at Agent Chase.

                    DETECTIVE JONES
          I found some very interesting
          information in the criminal
          database about two of her victims.
          They both have a criminal past of
          domestic violence and rape.

Agent Chase turns his head and looks at Detective Jones.

                    AGENT CHASE
          Are you serious?

Turning his head back to the road Agent Chase quickly glance
at his side and rear mirrors.

                    DETECTIVE JONES
          Yep, I think there's a connection
          on the victims she's choosing.

Focus on the road Agent Chase checks for cars, signs, and
traffic lights by keeping his eyes straight and moving them
left to right.

                    AGENT CHASE
          Well, spit it out.

Detective Jones nervously coughs looking at Agent Chase.

                    DETECTIVE JONES
              (Coughs Nervously)
          It's just a hunch now, I think all
          her victims got some type of
          criminal record or has a past, on
          abusing women.

Agent Chase glances at Detective Jones then looks at the
road.

(CONTINUED)

                          AGENT CHASE
                    So, your telling me she is some
                    damn vigilante?

Shrugging his shoulders, looking at Agent Chase, then turns
his head towards the road Detective Jones watches the
scenery that's around.

                          DETECTIVE JONES
                    Appear so, maybe it's just rage or
                    revenge. I don't know, but there's
                    a motive.

Looking straight ahead Agent Chase moves his head from left
to right.

                          AGENT CHASE
                    Revenge...revenge against who?

Turning his head to Agent Chase giving him a stern look
Detective Jones nonchalantly answers.

                          DETECTIVE JONES
                    Men.

Glancing at Detective Jones and the road shock by his
response Agent Chase shouts.

                          AGENT CHASE
                        (Shouts)
                    Are you fucking kidding me, we're
                    going to be fucking extinct?

Moving his head away from looking at Agent Chase to the
scenery Detective Jones calmly answers.

                          DETECTIVE JONES
                    If we don't catch her. It looks
                    like she's not stopping at all.

Agent Chase turns his head to Detective Jones then turns his
head back to the road.

                          AGENT CHASE
                    Fuck.

EXT. OUTSIDE - NIGHT - EVENING

A man in his late 20s chases a woman in her late 20s out of
the bar grabbing her and yelling at her. Victoria is walking
and watching from across the street. The man pushes the
woman to the ground, walks away, and signal/call for a cab.

                                                  (CONTINUED)

She runs across the street in seductive six inch heels. He
gets in the cab. The cab drives off Victoria walks to and
helps the woman off the ground.

                    VICTORIA
          Are you okay?

The woman stands on her feet and looks at Victoria.

                    BRITTANY
          Yeah, I'm okay.

Victoria points at the cab direction looking at Brittany
confused.

                    VICTORIA
          What about that guy?

Annoyed with her question Brittany side eyes Victoria.

                    VICTORIA
          I saw him push you from across the
          street.

Putting her head down from embarrassment Brittany slowly
moves her head up to look at Victoria in her eyes.

                    BRITTANY
          Fuck, I'm so embarrassed. That was
          nothing. He was a little tipsy.
          Don't worry about it, everything is
          cool. Where are my manners? My
          mother raised me better, Brittany
          Quinn.

Brittany extends her hand towards Victoria.

                    VICTORIA
          Tameka Albright.

Extending her hand as well Victoria and Brittany shakes
hands.

                    BRITTANY
          Nice to meet you.

They stop shaking each others hands and pull their hands
away from each other.

                    VICTORIA
          Nice to meet you.

In a chipper way Brittany smiles at Victoria.

                                        (CONTINUED)

                              BRITTANY
                    Thank you for your help.

Brittany hesitates a step then begins to walk.

                              VICTORIA
                    No problem.

Victoria begins to walk in another direction. Brittany stops
walking, turns, and looks at Victoria.

                              BRITTANY
                    Hey, do you want to grab a drink?

Hearing Brittany's voice from a distance Victoria stops
walking turns and looks at her.

                              VICTORIA
                    Sure.

INT. THE GREEN PUB - NIGHT - EVENING

Victoria and Brittany are sitting at the bar with shot
glasses in front of them. Brittany orders another round for
her and Victoria from the Bartender a male in his early 30s.

                              BRITTANY
                    Hey, Joe another round for me and
                    my friend.

The Bartender Joe looks at Brittany smiles and wink.

                              JOE
                    You got it.

Joe grabs two shot glasses places them in front of Victoria
and Brittany then grabs the dirty glasses. After putting the
dirty glasses away he grabs a bottle of Tequila and pours it
into the shot glasses. Brittany hands the Bartender twenty
dollars. Placing the bottle down on the bar he grabs the
twenty dollar bill out of Brittany's hand then walks away to
the cash register. Victoria and Brittany grab and drink the
shots of Tequila. They both place their shot glasses on the
bar.

                              VICTORIA
                    What's up with your boyfriend?

Brittany turns her head and looks at Victoria.

                              BRITTANY
                    Oh, him.

Disgusted by Victoria's question she rolls her eyes and
sighs.

                              BRITTANY
                         (Sighs)
                    He's a dick.

Confuse by Brittany's reaction moving her hands palms up
Victoria responds with a body gesture.

                              VICTORIA
                    So, why are you with him?

Looking up to the ceiling of the bar Brittany smiles in a
smitten way then looks back at Victoria.

                              BRITTANY
                    Because, I love him.

Nonchalantly Victoria looks and speaks to Brittany.

                              VICTORIA
                    Girl, love is blind, it's nothing,
                    but a second hand emotion.

Staring at Victoria shrugging her shoulders Brittany rolls
her eyes.

                              BRITTANY
                    I guess so.

Annoyed with Brittany's attitude Victoria is confused by her
actions.

                              VICTORIA
                    So you like being treated like
                    shit?

Turning away from Victoria looking straight ahead Brittany
closes her eyes and exhales.

                              BRITTANY
                         (Exhales)
                    It's not that I like it, it's just
                    all I know.

With a stern look Victoria stares at Brittany.

                                              (CONTINUED)

                         VICTORIA
                What if you kill him?

Opening her eyes Brittany turns her head to Victoria smiles
and laughs.

                         BRITTANY
                    (Smiles)
                I should ask the DB Slasher to kill
                his ass for me.

Brittany turns her head to Joe and points up with her index
finger.

                         BRITTANY
                Another one.

Joe nods his head acknowledging Brittany and her order.

                         VICTORIA
                The DB slasher?

Shock by Victoria's question Brittany slowly turns her head
to her.

                         BRITTANY
                Yeah the serial killer that's been
                all over the news.

Moving her head up and down Victoria responds quickly.

                         VICTORIA
                Yes I've heard of her, I just don't
                know why they call her the DB
                Slasher?

Smiling and laughing Brittany glances at Victoria.

                         BRITTANY
                DB Slasher means Dick Balls
                Slasher.

Victoria closes her eyes then opens them laughing.

                         VICTORIA
                    (Laughs)
                That's funny.

She stops laughing turns to Joe smiling. Joe hands Brittany
and Victoria another shots of Tequila. Brittany hands him a
twenty dollar bill. He grabs the money and walks away. They
grab the shot glasses and drinks them. Both of them places
their shot glasses on the bar at the same time.

                                              (CONTINUED)

                         BRITTANY
              Kill him, that never crossed my
              mind, like I told you I love him.
              He's been there since day one and
              he always going to be there.

Turning her head slowly to look at Brittany in a strong
demeanor tone Victoria speaks.

                         VICTORIA
              I tell you one thing he will be
              here, but you won't.

Instantly Brittany becomes afraid after listening to
Victoria.

INT. PRECINCT - DAY - AFTERNOON

Agent Chase and Detective Jones are walking down the
precinct hallway. They both see an Male Officer approaching
them.

                         OFFICER 1
              Hello Agent Chase, we have been
              expecting you.

Reaching his hand out to shake the officer's hand Agent
Chase turns his head to Detective Jones. The Officer looks
at Detective Jones while shaking Agent Chase's hand.

                         AGENT CHASE
              How are you doing, this is my
              partner Agent Jones.

Agent Chase and the Officer stop shaking hands pulling their
hands away from each other. Looking at Detective Jones the
Officer places his hand towards him.

                         OFFICER 1
              Please to meet you.

Detective Jones looks at the Officer then places his hand
out towards him. After shaking each other hands they both
places their hand by their side.

                         DETECTIVE JONES
              Please to meet you.

Watching the Officer and Detective Jones greet each other
Agent Chase looks at the Officer with arms folded.

                                              (CONTINUED)

                         AGENT CHASE
                    Did anyone find anything?

The Officer looks and speaks nervously at Agent Chase.

                         OFFICER 1
                    No sir nothing.

Unfolding his arms Agent Chase looks at the Officer, turns
and look at Detective Jones, then turns back to the Officer.

                         AGENT CHASE
                    Jones has a theory.

Curious about Detective Jones' theory the Officer looks at
Detective Jones with excitement.

                         OFFICER 1
                    Really?

Disturb by the way the Officer is looking at him quickly
glancing at Agent Chase back to the Officer Detective Jones
quickly responds.

                         DETECTIVE JONES
                    Yeah, I need to check your database
                    to see if the victim had any
                    priors.

Pointing down a hallway the Officer direct Detective Jones
to a location.

                         OFFICER 1
                    Okay, right this way.

The Officer walks away and Detective Jones follows.

Brittany walks into the apartment. Her boyfriend Josh is
sitting on the sofa in the living room watching a football
game on television.

                         JOSH
                    Who dat! Who dat!...who dat say
                    they gonna beat dem Saints. Let's
                    go Saints!

INT. BRITTANY'S APARTMENT - LIVING ROOM - DAY - EVENING

Josh turns his head away from the television and towards
Brittany.

                    JOSH
          Where the hell have you been?

INT. BRITTANY'S APARTMENT - DAY - EVENING

Hanging her coat and purse by the door way on the coat
hanger Brittany walks away from the front door and into the
living room with Josh.

INT. BRITTANY'S APARTMENT - LIVING ROOM - DAY - EVENING

Walking into the living room Brittany looks and sits next to
Josh on the sofa.

                    BRITTANY
          I was with Tameka, I told you about
          her.

Nonchalantly Josh looks and speaks to Brittany.

                    JOSH
          Oh, that hoe.

He turns his head back to the television.

                    BRITTANY
          She's not a hoe, she's my friend.

Jumping off the sofa Josh stands over and on top of Brittany
wrapping his hand around her neck/throat.

                    JOSH
          I'm your one and only fucking
          friend. Fuck that bitch.

Feeling the pressure from Josh's hand around her neck
Brittany starts sobbing, crying, and choking.

                    BRITTANY
                 (Choking)
          Josh, baby stop, you're hurting me.

Applying more pressure to her throat Josh looks at Brittany
and smiles.

                                              (CONTINUED)

                         JOSH
               You know, you like it.

Removing his hand off Brittany neck/throat he stands, sits
next to Brittany on the sofa and resume watching the game.

                         JOSH
               Come on, where's the fucking
               defense.

Curling up with fear on the sofa Brittany creates distance
between herself and Josh. Frustrated hearing Brittany crying
Josh raises his arm and points at her direction.

                         JOSH
               You better shut that shit up,
               before I silence your ass.

She cries quietly in the fetal position on the far side end
of the sofa.

                         JOSH
               Now that's better.

Watching the game Josh's jumps up and screams with
excitement.

                         JOSH
                    (Screams)
               Let's go Saints!

EXT./INT. VICTORIA'S APARTMENT - NIGHT

Victoria hears a knock at the door. She walks to the door
and opens it. Brittany is standing at the doorway crying.

                         VICTORIA
               Brittany, what's wrong?

Tears falling down her eyes Brittany is shaking with fear
standing in the door way.

                         BRITTANY
               Can I come in?

Concern with Brittany crying standing in front the door way
with the front door open. Putting her hand on Brittany's
shoulder comforting her Victoria looks at her with sympathy
in her eyes.

                                            (CONTINUED)

                         VICTORIA
              Of course come in.

Walking inside Victoria's apartment Brittany looks around
the apartment with tears. As she walks inside Victoria
removes her hand off her shoulder closing the front door.

INT. VICTORIA'S APARTMENT - LIVING ROOM - NIGHT

Brittany walks into the living room and sits on the sofa,
Victoria follows sitting next to her.

                         BRITTANY
              It's Josh, he got mad at me for
              hanging out with you, then out of
              nowhere he jumps on top of me and
              starts to choke me.

After listening to Brittany's story Victoria yells in anger.

                         VICTORIA
                    (Yells)
              He fucking did what?

Sitting on the sofa sobbing and crying Brittany places her
head down onto her arms and hands. Wrapping her arms around
Brittany calming her down Victoria softly pats her on the
back.

                         VICTORIA
              It's going to be okay.

Crying nonstop with tears falling down her face Brittany
buries her face in her lap.

                         BRITTANY
                    (Crying)
              What am I going to do? I love him.

Patting Brittany on her back Victoria unwraps her arm. Still
patting her back looking at Brittany a tear falls down
Victoria's facial cheek.

                         VICTORIA
              But, he doesn't love you. You can
              stay here tonight. Fresh towels are
              right there in the closet.

Pointing at the closet door Victoria wipes the tear off her
face.

                              VICTORIA
                    You can sleep in my room the bed is
                    real comfortable. It's right down
                    the hall to the left.

She points down the hallway, then stops pointing.

                              VICTORIA
                    I'll sleep on the couch.

Once she stops pointing Victoria Taps on the sofa/couch and
removes her hand off Brittany's back. Lifting her head up
from her lap and hands off her face Brittany looks at
Victoria.

                              BRITTANY
                    Are you sure?

Moving her head up and down Victoria looks around the
apartment, then back at Brittany.

                              VICTORIA
                    Yes, you are safe here.

Smiling at Victoria wiping the tears off her eyes Brittany
stops crying completely.

                              BRITTANY
                    Thank you.

Quickly hugging Victoria feeling very thankful Brittany
closes her eyes in relief.

                              VICTORIA
                    It's no problem sweetie.

Opening her eyes Brittany stops hugging Victoria.

                              BRITTANY
                    Where's your shower?

Victoria points to the hallway.

                              VICTORIA
                    Down the hall to the right.

Looking to where Victoria is pointing Brittany sees a door
way.

                              BRITTANY
                    Okay.

                                                   (CONTINUED)

Getting off the sofa Brittany walks to the closet, open the
closet door, then grabs a towel and wash cloth. Closing the
closet door she looks at Victoria.

                    BRITTANY
          Thanks again.

Brittany walks down the hallway to the bathroom door. She
opens the door, turn the lights on and proceed to walk
inside. Watching Brittany walk inside the bathroom and close
the door, sitting on the sofa Victoria stares down the
hallway with a evil grin on her face.

INT. VICTORIA'S APARTMENT - NIGHT - MIDNIGHT

Victoria looks through the crack of her bedroom door
watching Brittany sleep. She closes the door and exits.

INT. BRITTANY'S APARTMENT - NIGHT - MIDNIGHT

Picking the apartment door lock with a lock pick Victoria
opens the door. She walks inside the apartment and quietly
closes the door. Victoria is standing in a dark room with no
one in sight. Hearing keys jiggling on the front door she
quickly hides in the closet. Josh opens door standing in the
door way while kissing a beautiful woman in her mid 20s.
They both walk inside with there lips touching each other.
He closes the door and turns on the light. Kissing, hugging
and touching each other Josh and the woman walks to the sofa
in the living room.

INT. BRITTANY'S APARTMENT - LIVING ROOM - NIGHT - MIDNIGHT

They lay down on the sofa, the woman on the bottom and Josh
on top.

INT. BRITTANY'S APARTMENT - INSIDE CLOSET - NIGHT - MIDNIGHT

Victoria is listening and watching from the closet.

                    VICTORIA
          That fucking jerk.

INT. BRITTANY'S APARTMENT - LIVING ROOM - NIGHT - MIDNIGHT

With their clothes off and a blanket over their bodies. Josh
and the woman make moan noises while Josh is on top of the
woman performing up and down motions on her. He makes one
big moan then quickly gets off the woman.

                    JOSH
          Thank you. You can leave now.

The woman sits up with the blanket on her.

                    WOMAN 2
          Say what?

Grabbing her wrist Josh stands and pull the woman up.

                    JOSH
          You heard me.

Pulling her from the living room to the front door the woman
screams nonstop.

EXT. BRITTANY'S APARTMENT - FRONT DOOR - NIGHT - MIDNIGHT

Josh opens the door with his hand around the woman's arm. He
tosses her out of the apartment with no clothes on.

                    JOSH
          Get the fuck out!

Instantly he tosses all of her belongings out of the
apartment slamming the door.

Sfx: Door Slamming

                    WOMAN 2
          Fuck you!

The woman grabs all of her belongings and walks away.

INT. BRITTANY'S APARTMENT - LIVING ROOM - NIGHT - MIDNIGHT

Josh walks to the sofa and sits down.

INT. BRITTANY'S APARTMENT - INSIDE CLOSET - NIGHT - MIDNIGHT

Victoria watches every move Josh makes from the inside of
the closet.

INT. BRITTANY'S APARTMENT - LIVING ROOM - NIGHT - MIDNIGHT

Turning on the television he leans his head back and close
his eyes with the television on.

                                        FADE TO BLACK

                    VICTORIA
          Wakey-wakey.

With a Chef's Knife in her hand she pokes Josh in the leg
with the point of the blade. Tied up in a chair with rope
around his body Josh slowly opens his eyes.

                    JOSH
          You bitch, once I get my hands on
          you.

Applying more pressure to Josh's leg with the Chef's Knife
making Josh scream. She looks and picks up a random clothing
item with her hand. Taking that random clothing and shoving
it in Josh's mouth gagging him.

                    VICTORIA
          Be careful, I don't like people
          calling me that.

Victoria removes the knife off of Josh's leg.

                    VICTORIA
          So, you like putting your hands on
          women and disrespect them.

Staring into Josh's eyes removing the clothing slowly out of
his mouth Victoria stands with the Chef's Knife by her side.

                    JOSH
                 (Gags)
          What are you talking about,
          Brittany? I love that girl I would
          never do that.

Raising her voice Victoria yells at Josh.

                    VICTORIA
                 (Yells)
          I'm no fool!

                                        (CONTINUED)

Quickly placing the Chef's Knife to Josh's neck looking at him with rage in her eyes. Sitting in the chair shaking and trembling nervously frightened with a Chef's Knife at his neck Josh slowly glances at Victoria.

> VICTORIA
> I know, what you do to her and I
> will make sure you will never do it
> again.

Looking at Victoria with aggression Josh sit in the chair wiggling and moving through the tied up rope.

> JOSH
> Fuck you, bitch.

He spits at Victoria's face. She quickly grabs the clothing and shoves it back in his mouth.

> VICTORIA
> I told you I don't like when people
> call me that.

Victoria slits his neck/throat with the Chef's Knife in one quick motion. His blood falls down his chest onto the living room floor.

INT. VICTORIA'S APARTMENT - BED ROOM - NIGHT - MIDNIGHT

Brittany open her eyes and raises up.

> BRITTANY
> Tameka.

She gets out of the bed and walks out the room.

INT. VICTORIA'S APARTMENT - NIGHT - MIDNIGHT

> BRITTANY
> Tameka, are you here?

Walking around the apartment looking through cabinets, inspecting counter tops.

INT. VICTORIA'S APARTMENT - BATHROOM - NIGHT - MIDNIGHT

Walking into the bathroom Brittany stands in front of the medicine cabinet, opens the medicine cabinet door, looks through all Victoria's medicine products, then walks out of the bathroom.

INT. VICTORIA'S APARTMENT - NIGHT - MIDNIGHT

Strolling around the apartment Brittany sees and approaches
an unfamiliar door.

                    BRITTANY
          Hmmm...she never mention this room.

She touches and turns the door knob.

                    BRITTANY
          Wow it's locked.

Brittany bends down and places her eye through the door key
hole. Victoria appears out of nowhere watching her looking
through the key hole with a black duffel bag in her hand.

                    VICTORIA
          Looking for something?

Jumping in a state of shock Brittany sees Victoria appears
next to her out of nowhere.

                    BRITTANY
          Girl, you scared the shit out of
          me. Yeah I was looking for you.

Standing next to Brittany watching her stand up slowly
Victoria calmly speaks.

                    VICTORIA
          Well here I am.

Glancing at Victoria's hand holding a black duffel bag very
tightly Brittany wonders and questions.

                    BRITTANY
          What's in the bag?

Shrugging her shoulder nonchalantly Victoria grips the
duffel bag tighter.

                    VICTORIA
          It's just a souvenir.

Giving Brittany a evil stare Victoria slowly smiles
sadistically.

                    VICTORIA
          Is there anything else I can help
          you with?

Keeping her eyes on Victoria as she walks pass her at a slow
pace in fear Brittany calmly responds.

                                        (CONTINUED)

                         BRITTANY
                No, I'm going to just go back to
                bed. Goodnight.

Brittany walks faster pass Victoria towards the bed room
door.

                         VICTORIA
                Goodnight.

Victoria watches Brittany walk to and inside the bed room.

INT. VICTORIA'S APARTMENT - BED ROOM - DAY - MORNING

Opening her eyes, waking up, placing each foot down one by
one, Brittany gets off the bed, and walks out of the bed
room.

INT. VICTORIA'S APARTMENT - DAY - MORNING

Walking around the apartment seeing doors open and empty
closets and rooms Brittany yells throughout the apartment.

                         BRITTANY
                (Yells)
                Tameka!

Seeing a empty apartment Brittany looks down and sees a
piece of paper with words written down saying "You're Free
Now". Brittany is confuse reading the note.

INT. POLICE PRECINCT - OFFICE - DAY - AFTERNOON

Agent Chase walks into the office. He sees Detective Jones
sitting in a chair, on the computer, going through the
computer database and case files.

                         AGENT CHASE
                What did you find?

Watching Agent Chase from the corner of his eye walking
towards him. Detective Jones turns away from the computer
and looks at Agent Chase.

                         DETECTIVE JONES
                Just like I thought. Another
                criminal charge for domestic
                violence and assault.

Turning back to the computer Detective Jones points at the
monitor. Standing next to Detective Jones bending down Agent
Chase looks in the direction that Detective Jones is
pointing on the monitor.

> AGENT CHASE
> I'll be damn.

Agent Chase cell phone rings. He stands up, places his hand
in his pocket, grabs the phone, takes it out of his pocket,
and answers it. Placing the phone to his ear Agent Chase
glances at the computer monitor then looks away.

SFX: Cell Phone Ringing

> AGENT CHASE
> Chase. Are you shitting me, we're
> on the way.

Concern watching Agent Chase talking on the phone Detective
Jones ease drops on the conversation.

> DETECTIVE JONES
> What?

Agent Chase hangs up the phone and looks at Detective Jones.

> AGENT CHASE
> They found another body in the
> bayou. And guess, what he's
> missing?

Detective Jones grabs his belongings.

> DETECTIVE JONES
> Let's go.

Once Detective Jones walks pass and exits Agent Chase
instantly follows him.

> AGENT CHASE
> Let's go catch us a serial killer.

EXT. LOUISIANA BAYOU - DAY - AFTERNOON

Police officers, Investigators, and Forensics are all over
the bayou examining the dead male body and the crime scene.
Caution tape surrounds the entire crime scene. Agent Chase
and Detective Jones arrives to the crime scene. Approaching
a Patrol Man tapping him on the shoulder Agent Chase stands
next to him. The Patrol Man turns and looks and sees Agent
Chase next to him.

                        AGENT CHASE
              Whose the lead on this case?

Pointing to a middle age man in his mid 50s the Patrol Man
directs them. Agent Chase and Detective Jones walks towards
the middle age man. Standing next to the man Agent Chase
grabs his attention, introducing his self and Detective
Jones.

                        AGENT CHASE
              I'm Agent Chase from the FBI and
              this is Agent Jones.

Placing his hand out towards the middle age man for an
handshake. The man looks at Agent Chase, places his hand out
and shakes Agent Chase's hand. Agent Chase and the man stop
shaking hands and remove their hands away from each other.
Introducing his self to Agent Chase and Detective Jones
looking at both of them the man calmly speaks.

                        SERGEANT RODGERS
              I'm Sergeant Rodgers. I heard that
              you were chasing this killer.

Looking around the crime scene seeing all the Officers and
Forensics on the scene Agent Chase then looks at Sergeant
Rodgers.

                        AGENT CHASE
              I'm doing a whole lot of chasing,
              but I'm not getting anywhere. Hope
              you got something.

Sergeant Rodgers looks at the male and female officers that
are working on and around the crime scene.

                        SERGEANT RODGERS
              My men and women have been
              searching all day. We haven't find
              anything even his...

He turns and looks at Agent Chase.

                        AGENT CHASE
              We know, we know, the killer maybe
              collecting trophies.

Shock by Agent Chase statement Sergeant Rodgers eyes widens.

                        SERGEANT RODGERS
              Really? Collecting?

Covering his mouth with his hand Sergeant Rodgers coughs
into it, he grabs a handkerchief out of his pocket to wipe
his mouth.

                    SERGEANT RODGERS
                (Coughs)
            Excuse me.

Watching him cough Agent Chase becomes concern.

                    AGENT CHASE
            Are you okay?

Putting his handkerchief in his pocket Sergeant Rodgers
stops coughing.

                    SERGEANT RODGERS
            Yeah, I just got a little choke up.

Calmly responds Agent Chase puts his hands in his pants
pockets.

                    AGENT CHASE
            Dealing with a case like this, can
            do that for you. Here's my card.

Taking a business card out of his pants pocket Agent Chase
stretch his arm out and hands it to Sergeant Rodgers.
Placing his hand out towards Agent Chase he takes the
business card from him.

                    AGENT CHASE
            If you find anything, or have a
            lead call me.

Staring at the business card Sergeant Rodgers quickly
glances at Agent Chase.

                    SERGEANT RODGERS
            Yes sir.

Agent Chase and Detective Jones walks away and exits.

INT. BRITTANY'S APARTMENT - DAY - AFTERNOON

Brittany walks into the apartment.

                    BRITTANY
            Babe, you home we need to talk.

Walking around noticing her apartment has been clean
thoroughly. She worries and stresses looking for her
boyfriend throughout the apartment.

                              BRITTANY
                    Babe, babe are you home. Where the
                    fuck could he be.

Her cell phone rings.

SFX: Cell phone Ring tone

Grabbing her cell phone, answering it, and placing it on her
ear calmly speaking.

                              BRITTANY
                    Hello, yes this is she.

Sitting down on the floor Brittany cries and screams loudly.

                              BRITTANY
                           (Cry and Screams)
                    No! Are you serious. I'm on my way.

Ending the phone call Brittany stands up and exits the
apartment.

INT. MORGUE - DAY - EVENING

The Morgue Attendant flips the sheet to reveal the identity
to Sergeant Rodgers and Brittany. Recognizing the body
Brittany starts to cry uncontrollably.

                              BRITTANY
                    That's him, oh my god, it's him.

Seeing the dead body of her boyfriend Josh, Brittany has a
look of disbelief.

                           SERGEANT RODGERS
                    Ms. Davis are you okay?

Brittany looks at Sergeant Rodgers and screams while crying.

                              BRITTANY
                             (Screams)
                    It's him!

Sergeant Rodgers opens his arms up and hugs her for comfort
placing her head on Sergeant Rodgers chest she cries
nonstop. He looks at the Morgue Attendant.

                           SERGEANT RODGERS
                    Cover him up.

The Morgue Attendant covers the face and body of Josh's dead
body with the bed sheet.

INT. POLICE PRECINCT - DAY - EVENING

Sitting at his desk Sergeant Rodgers has the phone on his
ear.

                    SERGEANT RODGERS
              Chase, we got an id of the body.
              When you get a chance stop by the
              precinct. There's something I will
              like to talk to you about.

EXT./INT. CAR - FAST FOOD RESTAURANT - DAY - EVENING

Agent Chase is sitting in the car holding the phone to his
ear, waiting for Detective Jones to come out of a fast food
restaurant.

                    AGENT CHASE
              Okay, me and Jones are on our way.

Ending the phone call Agent Chase watches Detective Jones
opens the passenger seat door with bags of food in his
hands. He sits down in the passenger seat, places the bags
of food on the floor, then closes the passenger side door.
Watching his every movement Agent Chase calmly speaks.

                    AGENT CHASE
              That Officer at the crime scene
              just called me. He got an id of the
              body. That might lead us to
              something. He want us to meet him
              at his precinct.

Detective Jones looks at Agent Chase.

                    DETECTIVE JONES
              Why are we still here? Let's roll.

Agent Chase turns his head, look forward, and drives off.

EXT. POLICE PRECINCT - OUTSIDE - DAY - EVENING

Sergeant Rodgers is standing outside of the police precinct
waiting for Agent Chase and Detective Jones with a file in
his hand. Walking towards Sergeant Rodgers Detective Jones
and Agent Chase approaches him. Handing the file to Agent
Chase glancing around the area Sergeant Rodgers looks at him
open up the file.

                                        (CONTINUED)

                         SERGEANT RODGERS
                 The victim was named Josh McDaniel.
                 His girlfriend came by the Morgue
                 and id him a few hours ago.

Standing next to Agent Chase peeking over his shoulder
Detective Jones looks and read the file that's in his hand.

                         DETECTIVE JONES
                 Does he has a criminal background
                 of domestic abuse?

Putting his hands in his pockets Sergeant Rodgers looks at
Detective Jones.

                         SERGEANT RODGERS
                 Haven't check. Why would he?

Slowly grabbing the file from Agent Chase holding it looking
at the pages that's inside it Detective Jones carefully
reads with his eyes.

                         DETECTIVE JONES
                 We believe, our suspect is
                 attacking men with domestic
                 violence or rape charges.

Sergeant Rodgers express a sense of excitement.

                         SERGEANT RODGERS
                 Oh shit! We can call the girlfriend
                 for questioning maybe she can give
                 us some answers about his
                 background.

Agent Chase and Detective Jones both look at each other.

                         AGENT CHASE
                 Worth a shot.

INT. BRITTANY'S APARTMENT - DAY - EVENING

Brittany is sitting on the floor crying looking at
photograph pictures of herself and Josh. A piece of paper is
lying down on the floor a few inches away, she turns and
sees it. Reaching out towards the paper she grabs the piece
of paper and reads it.

                         BRITTANY
                 What the...

                                              (CONTINUED)

She looks at the pictures then she reads the note. Back and forth from the note to the pictures her eyes move. Her cell phone rings.

Sfx: Cell Phone Rings

Staring at the photograph picture and the note she answers the cell phone.

                    BRITTANY
          Hello, yeah this is she. Sure okay
          be there soon.

Looking straight ahead she ends the phone call in the state of shock.

INT. POLICE PRECINCT - INTERVIEW ROOM 1 - DAY - EVENING

Brittany is sitting in the police precinct interview room alone waiting. Sergeant Rodgers walks into the interview room and sits across from Brittany.

INT. POLICE PRECINCT - INTERVIEW ROOM 1A - DAY - EVENING

Agent Chase and Detective Jones watches the interrogation through the double glass mirror connected to another room next to the interview room.

INT. POLICE PRECINCT - INTERVIEW ROOM 1 - DAY - EVENING

Placing his hand on the table Sergeant Rodgers looks at Brittany.

                    SERGEANT RODGERS
          Ms. Davis, thank you for coming in
          to speak with us.

She looks at Sergeant Rodgers with certainty in her eyes and confidence in her voice.

                    BRITTANY
          I know who killed Josh.

INT. POLICE PRECINCT - INTERVIEW ROOM 1A - DAY - EVENING

Smiling looking through the double glass mirror Agent Chase and Detective Jones are shock and surprise by Brittany's statement.

                                              (CONTINUED)

                    AGENT CHASE
          Oh shit, we got her.

INT. POLICE PRECINCT - INTERVIEW ROOM 1 - DAY - EVENING

Shock and surprise by Brittany statement Sergeant Rodgers
taps the table with his hand in excitement.

                    SERGEANT RODGERS
          What do you mean, you know who
          killed Josh?

Glancing down at the floor slowly looking at Sergeant
Rodgers.

                    BRITTANY
          I met this woman her name is Tameka
          Albright. I told her about an
          incident that happened between Josh
          and I. She let me stay the night at
          her home until things settle. When
          I woke up everything was gone. The
          only thing left was my clothes and
          the bed I was laying on, but there
          was a note she left me.

Brittany takes the note out of her pocket and slides on the
table towards Sergeant Rodgers. Putting his hand on top of
the note he slides it off the table into his hand. He takes
the note, looks at it, and reads it.

                    SERGEANT RODGERS
          What do she mean your free now?

A tear falls down Brittany's face.

                    BRITTANY
          Josh, physically and verbally abuse
          me throughout our entire
          relationship. I told her all about
          it.

Wiping the tear from her eye Brittany drops her head.

INT. POLICE PRECINCT - INTERVIEW ROOM 1A - DAY - EVENING

Detective Jones looks at Agent Chase.

                    DETECTIVE JONES
          There's the connection, we found
          her.

Agent Chase looks at Detective Jones and smiles.

INT. POLICE PRECINCT - INTERVIEW ROOM 1 - DAY - EVENING

Looking away from the note Sergeant Rodgers looks at
Brittany confuse.

>   SERGEANT RODGERS
>   So, why not call the cops and get
>   him arrested?

Water builds up in her eyes while staring at Sergeant
Rodgers.

>   BRITTANY
>   Because I love him.

Nonchalantly sitting in the chair Sergeant Rodgers leans
back looking at Brittany.

>   SERGEANT RODGERS
>   Okay, if she freed you, why come
>   here with this information that
>   could give her life or maybe the
>   chair?

She jumps out her seat and screams in anger.

>   BRITTANY
>   (Screams)
>   She killed the man I love. Justice
>   needs to be serve!

Sitting back in the chair Brittany calms down and begins to
cry. Sergeant Rodgers hands Brittany a box of tissues.

>   SERGEANT RODGERS
>   Okay. Excuse me for a moment, Ms.
>   Davis.

He stands up, glances at Brittany, then exits the interview
room.

INT. POLICE PRECINCT - INTERVIEW ROOM 1A - DAY - EVENING

Sergeant Rodgers walks into the room and stands next to
Agent Chase and Detective Jones.

>   SERGEANT RODGERS
>   We got her ass.

(CONTINUED)

Agent Chase and Detective Jones both smile at the same time.
Placing his hand on Detective Jones shoulder with a stern
look on his face Agent Chase gives him detail instructions.

                    AGENT CHASE
                 (Smiles)
            Jones, check that name in the
            computer database, I want birth
            certificate, Passports, Social
            Security number, address, her
            parents' address, her mother's and
            father's parents' address. Phone
            numbers from best friend to best
            uncle, auntie, and cousins. I want
            records mental and health, if she
            has a boyfriend or husband I want
            all his shit too.

Detective Jones looks at Agent Chase and nods his head.

                    DETECTIVE JONES
            On it.

He quickly exits the room. Getting a step closer to Agent
Chase grabbing his attention Sergeant Rodgers grin while
looking at him.

                    SERGEANT RODGERS
            What do you want me to do?

In a stern and confident way Agent Chase looks at Sergeant
Rodgers and demand.

                    AGENT CHASE
            Get all the information you can
            from her, she's our lead now.
            Whatever info she has about our
            suspect will help.

Sticking out his chest Sergeant Rodgers proudly responds and
salutes to Agent Chase.

                    SERGEANT RODGERS
            I'm on it.

He exits the room. Turning back to and looking through the
double mirror Agent Chase continues to watch Sergeant
Rodgers interviewing Brittany.

INT. POLICE PRECINCT - INTERVIEW ROOM - DAY - EVENING

Sergeant Rodgers enters the room and sits in the chair
across from Brittany.

                    SERGEANT RODGERS
            Tell me everything about her.

INT. BAR - NIGHT - EVENING

Victoria is sitting at the bar dress seductively with a
glass of champagne in front of her. Two police officers
walks into the bar. They sit at the bar a few seats away
from her. The Police Officers order drinks. She turns and
looks at the Officers sips her Champagne, pays the
Bartender, then exits the bar.

INT. POLICE PRECINCT - NIGHT - EVENING

Detective Jones is sitting at a desk, looking and searching
on the internet on the computer. Agent Chase taps his
shoulder to gets his attention.

                    AGENT CHASE
            What did you find out?

He turns away from the computer and looks at Agent Chase.

                    DETECTIVE JONES
            Nothing, I've checked everything,
            even with your access to the FBI
            database nothing. It's like Tameka
            Albright does not exist.

Grabbing a chair placing it next to Detective Jones, sitting
in it Agent Chase looks at the computer and all of Detective
Jones research.

                    AGENT CHASE
            Maybe she doesn't exist.

Looking at Agent Chase confuse sitting in his chair
Detective Jones questions.

                    DETECTIVE JONES
            What do you mean? Do you think, she
            created that identity?

Turning away from the computer and the research he looks at
Detective Jones grinning happily.

(CONTINUED)

                         AGENT CHASE
                    Think about it, if you have been
                    killing and brutally murdering over
                    state lines would you reveal people
                    your real identity? I bet she has
                    does this more than once. Maybe
                    that's one of the reasons she is
                    able to blend in so well from state
                    to state.

Frustrated Detective Jones balls his fist and hits the desk
on the bottom part of his hand.

                         DETECTIVE JONES
                    So we're back to square one?

Standing up off the chair Agent Chase smiles.

                         AGENT CHASE
                        (Smiles)
                    No, we are getting closer.

Watching Agent Chase stand up Detective Jones sits in his
chair confuse.

                         DETECTIVE JONES
                    How?

Winking at Detective Jones in a confident tone Agent Chase
answers.

                         AGENT CHASE
                    We will, find out who she is.

Unsure and confuse looking at Agent Chase raising his
eyebrow Detective Jones questions.

                         DETECTIVE JONES
                    You think so?

Placing his hand on Detective Jones shoulder Agent Chase
looks into his eyes with a smile on his face.

                         AGENT CHASE
                    I know so, she's getting cocky and
                    is beginning to make mistakes. We
                    just got to be patient, because she
                    will make another one, don't worry.

Removing his hand off Detective Jones shoulder Agent Chase
stands, turns, and walks away.

INT. HOTEL - NIGHT - EVENING

Victoria is sitting on the hotel bed in the dark. She grabs her cell phone, dial numbers on it, then place the phone to her ear.

                                                    INTER CUT

INT. WILLIAMS HOME - NIGHT - EVENING

Mrs. Williams hears the phone ringing. She answers the phone.

                    MRS. WILLIAMS
          Hello.

INT. HOTEL - NIGHT - EVENING

Sitting on the bed Victoria wipes a tear from her eye.

                    VICTORIA
          Hey mama.

INT. WILLIAMS HOME - LIVING ROOM - NIGHT - EVENING

Questioning the call Mrs. Williams takes a deep breathe walking in her living room turning on the light.

                    MRS. WILLIAMS
          Victoria?

INT. HOTEL - NIGHT - EVENING

As a tear fall down her face Victoria smile.

                    VICTORIA
          Yeah it's me.

INT. WILLIAMS HOME - LIVING ROOM - NIGHT - EVENING

Excited hearing Victoria's voice sitting on her living room sofa Mrs. Williams smile.

                    MRS. WILLIAMS
          Girl! I've been worried sick about
          you. It's been almost two years
          since I've heard from you.

INT. HOTEL - NIGHT - EVENING

Wiping a tear off her cheek Victoria chuckle.

                    VICTORIA
          I know. I'm okay. I just needed to
          hear your voice.

INT. WILLIAMS HOME - LIVING ROOM - NIGHT - EVENING

Leaving the living room Mrs. Williams walks towards the
kitchen.

INT. WILLIAMS HOME - KITCHEN - NIGHT - EVENING

Turning on the kitchen light Mrs. Williams walks towards the
refrigerator.

                    MRS. WILLIAMS
          Victoria, what's wrong baby?

INT. HOTEL - NIGHT - EVENING

Looking down at the floor Victoria places her hand on her
forehead.

                    VICTORIA
          Nothing mama.

Mrs. Williams opens the refrigerator and stands in front of
it with her hand on the door.

                    MRS. WILLIAMS
          Why, don't you come home baby?

Moving her hand back and forth rubbing her forehead Victoria
sobs and cries.

                    VICTORIA
              (Sobs)
          I can't mama, I can never come back
          home.

Closing the refrigerator door Mrs. Williams walks towards
the kitchen table.

                    MRS. WILLIAMS
          Well, when you're ready your father
          and I will be here waiting for you.
          We love you sweetheart we miss you

                                        (CONTINUED)

Victoria sniffs and wipes her tears.

                    VICTORIA
          I miss you guys too. I got to go
          mama thanks for the talk I love
          you. Give dad a hug and kiss for
          me.

Sitting down in the chair. Holding the phone she lightly
leans on the kitchen table.

                    MRS. WILLIAMS
          I love you too baby. I will bye.

Taking a deep breathe Victoria wipes a tear from her eyes
and cries silently.

                    VICTORIA
               (Silent Cry)
          Bye mama.

Ending the phone call Mrs. Williams wipes a tear off her
eye.

INT. HOTEL - NIGHT - EVENING

Victoria ends the phone call. Glancing at the nightstand
seeing her Chef's Knife on top of it. She grabs and holds
the knife in her hand leaning back on the bed she express a
sense of relief.

INT. COFFEE SHOP - DAY - MORNING

Agent Chase is sitting at a table with a Coffee mug on top
of it. Sergeant Rodgers walks inside the Coffee Shop and
approaches the table that Agent Chase is sitting at.

                    AGENT CHASE
          Have a seat.

He sits in the chair across from him, Agent Chase sits and
watches Sergeant Rodgers.

                    AGENT CHASE
          So...

An attractive waitress in her early 20s walks to the table
with a Coffee pot in her hand. Pouring the Coffee in Agent
Chase's Coffee cup she smiles at Agent Chase and Sergeant
Rodgers. Both of them glances at the waitress pouring the
Coffee smiling at her, Sergeant Rodgers looks back at Agent

Chase seriously. The waitress walks away from the table with
the Coffee pot in her hand.

                    SERGEANT RODGERS
               Nothing for real, mainly. The only
               thing that stood out to me in her
               statement. Was...

Sipping his Coffee then placing it softly on the table Agent
Chase looks at him.

                    AGENT CHASE
               What?

Putting his hands on top of the table Sergeant Rodgers makes
hand gestures.

                    SERGEANT RODGERS
               She said, "when she woke up every
               thing was gone including the
               furniture." So we know she fled and
               disappeared like that for a reason.

Sarcastically Agent Chase responds and smirks.

                    AGENT CHASE
               Yeah, she's the killer, but the
               only thing we don't know who the
               hell she is.

EXT. OUTSIDE - DAY - AFTERNOON

Victoria is wearing a form fitting dress with high heels
walking down the side walk. Two adult men in their mid 20s
walks by Victoria and screams inappropriate comments at her.

                    MAN 4
               Look at that ass right there.

Man 5 rolls his tongue looking at Victoria.

                    MAN 5
               Can I get a taste of that thang.

She stops and turns and give the two men an evil stare.

                    VICTORIA
               Be careful, what you wish for boys,
               because you might just get it.

Licking his lips looking at Victoria making inappropriate
gestures at her, Man 5 smiles seductively.

                              MAN 5
                         Baby I want it.

Frighten by her stare Man 4 lips and hands tremble. He looks
at Man 5 and whispers.

                              MAN 4
                         (Whispers)
                         Brother, you see that look she gave
                         us you can have it, that bitch is
                         crazy.

Victoria approaches Man 4 very aggressively.

                              VICTORIA
                         What did you just call me?

He turns his head looking at Man 5 with fear in his eyes
then quickly turn his head to Victoria nervously putting his
hands up.

                              MAN 4
                         (Nervous)
                         See, ma'am I'm sorry, I apologize
                         for my comments my mother raised me
                         better than that so, I'm going to
                         just roll out.

Looking at Man 4 staring with no facial expression Victoria
calms down. Man 5 looks Victoria up and down admiring her
physique.

                              MAN 5
                         Shit I'm not, I'm trying to spread
                         that kitty out.

Slowly turning his head with his mouth open shock by Man 5
actions making hand gestures Man 4 whispers.

                              MAN 4
                         (Whispers)
                         You be the fool, she's off the
                         wall, and I'm feeling some thriller
                         in my shiver. You can be with her
                         alone, I'm just going to beat it.

Confuse looking at Man 4 waving his hand Man 5 rolls his
eyes.

                              MAN 5
                         Whatever, I catch you later.

Whispering Man 4 try to convince Man 5 to exit with him
using body gestures.

                                                (CONTINUED)

                              MAN 4
                         (Whispers)
                    You sure.

Annoyed with Man 4 and his body gestures Man 5 whispers to
him.

                              MAN 5
                         (Whispers)
                    Yeah, I'm going to get her numerals
                    and I'll call you later.

Worry about Man 5 slowly and nervously responding Man 4
whispers back.

                              MAN 4
                         (Whispers)
                    Okay man.

Giving each other a handshake Man 4 and Man 5 looks at each
other with different emotions one happy(Man 5)the other
afraid(Man 4). After they stop shaking hands instantly Man 5
walks up to Victoria very smooth and suave.

                              MAN 5
                    So, can I get your number. We can
                    link up later. You like seafood?

Victoria looks at Man 4 with an demonic grin. He looks at
Victoria becoming frighten while exiting.

                              VICTORIA
                    Sure, I love seafood.

She quickly looks at Man 5 and smiles. He hands Victoria his
cell phone.

                              MAN 5
                    I know this great place. That makes
                    the best seafood in town.

Grabbing and holding his cell phone in her hand pressing
numbers on the phone's key pad she smiles and flirts with
him.

                              VICTORIA
                    Okay, just call me with the
                    details.

As she hands back Man 5 cell phone in his hand with lust in
his eyes he looks at Victoria.

                                                       (CONTINUED)

                              MAN 5
             I will.

Turning away from Man 5 walking away with a real dark evil
smile Victoria licks her lips seductively.

                           VICTORIA
             Okay, bye.

Starting to walk away she quickly glances at Man 5 waving.

                           VICTORIA
             Make sure you call.

She exits, Man 5 watches Victoria walk away.

                              MAN 5
             I think, I'm in love.

INT. HOTEL - DAY - MORNING

Agent Chase is laying down on the hotel bed with his eyes
closed. He hears the cell phone ringing. Grabbing his phone
he slowly opens his eyes, answering it in a groggy voice.

SFX: Cell Phone Ring Tone

                         AGENT CHASE
                       (Groggy Voice)
             Hello.

                                                    INTERCUT

INT. FBI HEADQUATERS - DIRECTOR OF FBI OFFICE - DAY -
MORNING

An 60 year old male is sitting at his desk with pictures of
his family that are place in picture frames. All of his
accolades and Degrees and Certificates are placed all over
the office walls. The man sits at the desk with a phone
place on his ear.

                        DIRECTOR WILSON
             Chase, I just got a call from
             Little Rock another murder same
             pattern. I need you there since
             yesterday.

INT. HOTEL - DAY - MORNING

Clearing his throat Agent Chase sits up on the bed with the comforter laid over his lap.

                    AGENT CHASE
          I'm already there Chief.

Director Wilson spin a inch in his chair.

                    DIRECTOR WILSON
          One thing, Chase before you go.

Removing the phone from his ear slowly Agent Chase quickly put the phone back to his ear to answer Director Wilson.

                    AGENT CHASE
          Yes sir.

In a stern voice Director Wilson speaks.

                    DIRECTOR WILSON
          There's DNA.

Ending the phone call Director Wilson looks straight ahead.

INT. POLICE PRECINCT - FORENSICS LABORATORY - DAY -
AFTERNOON

Agent Chase and Detective Jones walks into the Forensics lab. A male Lab tech in his mid 30s is examining under a microscope.

                    AGENT CHASE
          I'm FBI Agent Chase and this is
          Agent Jones. I heard you got some
          DNA?

The Lab Tech lifts his head up away from the microscope and looks at them.

                    LAB TECH
          Hi. My Captain told me you two were
          coming. You've been chasing this
          killer for awhile.

In a nonchalant way Agent Chase looks at the Lab Tech.

                    AGENT CHASE
          Yes we have, an this right here
          could be the key to put her away.
          So what do you got?

                                        (CONTINUED)

Responding with excitement the Lab Tech looks at Agent
Chase.

                    LAB TECH
          Saliva!

Shock and surprise standing proper Detective Jones responds
placing hands on his hips slightly leaning.

                    DETECTIVE JONES
          Get the fuck out of here.

Looking at Detective Jones the Lab Tech points at his lips.

                    LAB TECH
          Yep right all over the victim's
          lips.

Listening to the Lab Tech statement made Detective Jones
wonder and question.

                    DETECTIVE JONES
          How, do you know it's someone
          else's and not his?

Sarcastically answering Detective Jones making body gestures
the Lab Tech looks at him and smirks.

                    LAB TECH
          Unless he was kissing him self,
          someone was making out with him
          saliva was all over his lips.

Agent Chase grabs the Lab tech microscope towards him and
places his eyes on the eye piece.

                    AGENT CHASE
          Well do you know who the saliva
          belongs to?

Quickly grabbing the microscope away from Agent Chase
aggressively the Lab Tech stares at him. Backing away from
the microscope Agent Chase reacts to the action of the Lab
Tech.

                    LAB TECH
          Not yet I just started examining
          it, but once I figure it out. I'll
          let you know.

Reaching in his pocket Agent Chase pulls out his business
card.

                         AGENT CHASE
                    Okay cool.

Handing the Lab tech his business card Agent Chase stretches
his arm out towards him.

                         AGENT CHASE
                    Here's my card, call once you find
                    out anything. We need to put this
                    psycho in a padded room, not
                    roaming the earth free.

Taking Agent Chase's business card the Lab Tech nods his
head.

                         LAB TECH
                    I agree.

Putting his arm by his side Agent Chase looks at Detective
then they exit the Forensics Laboratory at the same time.

INT. POLICE PRECINCT - HALLWAY - DAY - AFTERNOON

Agent Chase and Detective Jones sees Two male officers in
their mid 30s escorting a man in his mid 20s that's crying
and screaming out of the precinct.

                         MAN 4
                    She killed my best friend!

Officer 2 raises his hand up towards Man 4.

                         OFFICER 2
                    Calm down sir.

Man 4 points his right index finger in the chest of Officer2
and yells at him.

                         MAN 4
                    Fuck you, she killed my best
                    friend!

Agent Chase and Detective Jones both look at each other.
They quickly approach the two officers and Man 4
deescalating the tension.

                         AGENT CHASE
                    Hey, I'm Agent Chase of the FBI and
                    this is Agent Jones.

Standing still without flinching Officer 2 looks down at
Man4 index finger. Turning his head looking at Agent Chase
with no facial expression. Removing his index finger off
Officer 2 chest, slowly turning his head Man 4 looks at
Agent Chase.

                    OFFICER 2
              How are you doing? Sir.

Nodding his head at Officer 2 quickly Agent Chase glances at
the officer then at Man 4 placing his hand on his shoulder.

                    AGENT CHASE
              Can I speak with this gentle man
              for a minute?

Shrugging their shoulders the officers looks at each other.

                    OFFICER 2
              Sure.

The two Officers walks away and exits. In an aggressive tone
Agent Chase speaks to Man 4.

                    AGENT CHASE
              Let me ask you this, did you see
              her?

Screaming and yelling at Agent Chase staring at him in anger
Man 4 becomes hostile.

                    MAN 4
                 (Screams and Yells)
              Of course I saw that crazy bitch, I
              can tell you what she look like.

With both of his hands Man 4 grabs onto Agent Chase's lapel
pulling him aggressively staring into his eyes.

                    MAN 4
              You ever seen evil in the face?

Counter attacking with his hands in a relax and calm way
Agent Chase's removes Man 4 hands off his lapel.

                    AGENT CHASE
              No.

Quickly calming down Man 4 glances at both Agent Chase and
Detective Jones. Holding and nurturing his hands once Agent
Chase lets go of them.

                         MAN 4
                Ow, Well that's fucking her.

Folding his arms Detective Jones looks at Man 4 speaking in
an authoritative tone.

                    DETECTIVE JONES
                So you can identify her?

Eyes wide open Man 4 looks and stares at Detective Jones.

                         MAN 4
                Fuck yeah, fucking evil.

Grabbing Man 4's arm to get his attention Agent Chase speaks
in an aggressive tone.

                      AGENT CHASE
                   (Aggressive Tone)
                No seriously, can you?

Releasing his arm Agent Chase places his hand by his side.
Man 4 turns his head and looks at Agent Chase then looks at
Detective Jones.

                         MAN 4
                Yes I can. If you need my help, say
                no more. She killed and brutally
                murdered my best friend and she
                deserve to be behind bars.

Anxiously Man 4 looks at Agent Chase and Detective Jones.
Reacting to Man 4's actions standing in a relax way Agent
Chase calms him down.

                      AGENT CHASE
                Okay, cool.

Detective Jones turns his head to look at Agent Chase then
looks at Man 4. Smiling Man 4 looks at Detective Jones and
Agent Chase standing still and attentive.

                         MAN 4
                What do you need me to do fellas?

Turning to look at each other Agent Chase and Detective
Jones both smile. Agent Chase and Detective Jones at the
same time turn their heads towards Man 4 still smiling.

INT. POLICE PRECINCT - INTERVIEW ROOM - DAY - AFTERNOON

Sitting in two chairs Agent Chase and Detective Jones sits
across the table from Man 4 staring and questioning him.

                    AGENT CHASE
          First, tell us how did you see her?

Putting his hands on the table making hand gestures on it
Man 4 looks at Agent Chase calmly answering him.

                    MAN 4
          Well me and my best friend...

Interested in the story Agent Chase questions in a
sympathetic tone.

                    AGENT CHASE
          The person that she just murdered?

A tear falls down Man 4 right cheek. Hopping out of the
chair slamming his hand on the table he expresses his anger
in a violent way.

                    MAN 4
          Yeah, that crazy
          bit...murderrr...my...

Slowly sitting back down in the chair Man 4 calms him self
down into a relax state.

                    MAN 4
          Phew, calm down, well my best
          friend and I was walking heading to
          the corner store in my
          neighborhood. I admit she's
          beautiful and a body out of this
          world, but the light in her eyes is
          gone straight pure darkness. I told
          him to leave her alone. But he
          didn't want to listen to me. He has
          to talk to every woman that he
          sees.

Detective Jones smirks and giggles looking at Man 4. He
leans and whispers in Agent Chase's ear.

                    DETECTIVE JONES
                    (Whispers)
          Yeah, I bet he wish he would've
          passed this one up.

Laughing quietly Agent Chase leans and whispers in Detective
Jones ear.

                                        (CONTINUED)

                         AGENT CHASE
                        (Whispers)
                You can say that again.

Once Agent Chase sees Man's 4 sad face he instantly stop
laughing.

                         AGENT CHASE
                Sorry for that.

Looking at Agent Chase then quickly turning to look at Man 4
with no expression Detective Jones questions.

                         DETECTIVE JONES
                Let me ask you this, did your
                friend have a record for domestic
                violence or any type of charges of
                abuse towards women?

Hitting his hands on top of the desk slamming it up and down
Man 4 raises his voice.

                         MAN 4
                        (Raises Voice)
                I'm tell you this he might talk to
                or fuck any woman he can get his
                eyes on. Abusing women? Is not his
                thing.

Lowering his voice inhaling and exhaling Man 4 calms down
slowly.

                         MAN 4
                        (Inhales, Exhales)
                He may call a woman a bitch or hoe
                in her face, but abuse is not his
                thing.

Placing his right hand on his chin Man 4 sits in the the
chair in a daze.

                         MAN 4
                Shit that might of what pissed her
                off.

Smacking the table with his right hand Detective Jones rocks
in the chair.

                         DETECTIVE JONES
                And there's the pattern.

Glancing around the room, at Man 4 and at Detective Jones
shock with his mouth open Agent Chase softly speaks.

                                              (CONTINUED)

                         AGENT CHASE
               I'll be damn, the fucking motive.

Man 4 folds his arms and leans back in the chair.

                         MAN 4
               So now you know this bitch is crazy
               and she's the one that killed my
               friend can we go get her ass and
               put her evil ass behind some walls,
               bars, or something away from all of
               us and let her evil ass be by her
               fucking self.

Agent Chase and Detective Jones looks at Man 4 then at each
other.

INT. BIANCA'S SEXY BOUTIQUE - DAY - EVENING

Victoria is walking around a boutique clothing store looking
at seductive sexy lingerie. A woman in her early twenties
approaches Victoria.

                         BOUTIQUE WORKER
               Do you need any help? Ma'am!

She stops looking at the lingerie and turns to the Boutique
worker.

                         VICTORIA
               No, I'm fine. I'm just looking
               right now.

The Boutique worker looks at Victoria and smiles.

                         BOUTIQUE WORKER
               If you need any help please let me
               know.

Smiling Victoria looks at the Boutique Worker watching her
walk away. Walking away the Boutique Worker smiles and looks
at the other customers that are inside the Boutique.

                         VICTORIA
               Okay.

Victoria continues to look at the lingerie. Sliding the
clothes on the clothing rack repeatedly,she sees two women
walk inside the Boutique, they begin to stare at Victoria.
Grabbing an outfit off the clothing rack she walks to the
check out counter. Taking the outfit to the counter and
placing it the outfit on the counter top, she hands the

cashier the amount of money that the outfit cost. The
Cashier/Boutique Worker takes the money and put it in the
cash register.

                    BOUTIQUE WORKER
            You have a good day ma'am.

Putting the outfit in a plastic bag the Cashier/Boutique
Worker hands the receipt and bag to Victoria.

                    VICTORIA
            Thank you, you do the same.

Victoria grabs the plastic bag and exits.

INT. COFFEE SHOP - DAY - EVENING

Man 4 just purchase a cup of coffee at the check out
counter. The Cashier hands Man 4 his change for the
purchase. Man 4 takes the change and walk towards the door.

EXT. COFFEE SHOP - OUTSIDE - DAY - EVENING

He walks outside the Coffee Shop and looks across the street
and sees Victoria standing with plastic bags in her hands.
Quickly grabbing his cell phone out of his pocket. Pressing
the numbers on the device then placing it on his ear with a
rapid tongue Man 4 speaks.

                    MAN 4
            Hey, Chase it's me I'm looking at
            her right now.

Victoria turns her head to the left then turns her head to
the right. She looks straight ahead and see Man 4 across the
street. Looking straight ahead Man 4 locks eyes with
Victoria.

                    MAN 4
            Oh shit, she's looking right at me.

Giving him an evil stare from across the street she smiles
slowly. A bus passes by Victoria. After the bus passes by
Victoria in a instant she disappears.

                    MAN 4
            Oh shit she fucking disappeared.

Appearing out of nowhere Victoria stands next to Man 4 on
the left side of his body.

                         VICTORIA
                 Who are you talking to?

Man 4 jumps out of fear once he sees Victoria. He removes
the phone away from his ear.

                         MAN 4
                 Oh shit, Who I'm talking to? Just
                 my mother. Have you seen Harvey
                 I've been calling him all day. I
                 know you guys went out the other
                 night.

Staring into Man 4's eyes speaking in an aggressive tone
Victoria moves her head from side to side.

                         VICTORIA
                 Oh yeah, Harvey that fucking handsy
                 perv couldn't keep his hand off me,
                 forcing me to kiss him. Worst date
                 of my life.

Nervously Man 4 shakes, tremble, and coughs looking at
Victoria.

                         MAN 4
                     (Coughs)
                 Really?

Watching Man 4 cover his mouth as he coughs over and over
again Victoria frowns her face. He stops coughing after his
third cough.

                         VICTORIA
                 Yes, really, but besides that I
                 don't know where he is and don't
                 want to know.

Sweating slowly down his forehead fearfully and anxious Man4
looks up and down Victoria's body. Looking at Victoria, the
bag she's carrying, and watching people pass by he instantly
gets nervous.

                         MAN 4
                 Well it was good seeing you.

Starting to walk away from Victoria quickly glancing Man 4
looks at her then looks straight ahead. She grabs Man 4 left
arm stopping his movement.

                         VICTORIA
                 Where are you going?

He points to his phone with his left index finger.

MAN 4
                I got to go my mom needs my help.

Taking her hand off Man 4 left arm Victoria stares at him
with an evil grin on her face.

VICTORIA
                Okay, you be safe don't want
                anything to happen to you.

Calmly looking at Victoria waving his hand Man 4 proceeds to
walk away.

MAN 4
                Okay, bye.

Placing the phone back to his ear Man 4 walks across the
street away from Victoria. Victoria stands and watches Man 4
walk away.

MAN 4
                I'm on my way.

EXT. OUTSIDE - DAY - EVENING

Man 4 is standing in a deserted area. Detective Jones and
Agent Chase drives up to Man 4 they stop the car and turned
it off. They both steps out of the car, close the car doors,
and walks towards Man 4.

AGENT CHASE
                What happen? Are you okay?

Seeing Detective Jones and Agent Chase walking towards him
meeting them half way he looks at Agent Chase shaking with
fear.

MAN 4
                Man she's pure evil.

Looking at Man 4 with his hand in his pockets Detective
Jones questions.

DETECTIVE JONES
                Well did you find out anything?

Calming him self down Man 4 looks at Detective Jones and
speaks in a relax tone.

MAN 4
                I was to scared, but I did notice
                she had a bag in her hand from
                Bianca's Sexy Boutique.

Detective Jones and Agent Chase both look at each other.

INT. BIANCA'S SEXY BOUTIQUE - DAY - EVENING

Detective Jones and Agent Chase walks inside the Boutique
and walk to the check out counter. Agent Chase shows and
flashes his FBI Badge at the Boutique Worker.

                    AGENT CHASE
          We need to see your Manager.

He put his Badge back in his pocket.

                    BOUTIQUE WORKER
          Sure, wait just a moment please.

They both stand and wait patiently for the Boutique Worker
and the Manager. The Manger a male in his late 40s and the
Boutique Worker returns to the check out counter.

                    MANAGER 3
          How may I help you gentlemen?

Pointing at the security camera in the Boutique Agent Chase
looks and the Manager and responds.

                    AGENT CHASE
          We need to see your Security
          footage.

In a suspicious way the Manager looks at Agent Chase and
questions.

                    MANAGER 3
          What is this concerning?

Cutting off the Manager quickly responding Detective Jones
speaks with an sarcastic tone.

                    DETECTIVE JONES
          A loose serial killer.

Shock the Manager gasp holding their chest.

                    MANAGER 3
          Are you serious in my store?

Giving the Manager of the store a stern look Agent Chase
leans on the counter towards the Manager.

(CONTINUED)

                         AGENT CHASE
                That's why we're here to find out.

The Manager points to a direction.

                         MANAGER 3
                Okay, follow me this way.

He stops pointing and exits walking towards the direction he
pointed to, Agent Chase and Detective Jones follows.

INT. BIANCA'S SEXY BOUTIQUE - SECURITY CAMERA ROOM - DAY -
EVENING

The Manager opens the Security Camera room door. Agent
Chase, Detective Jones, and the Manager are standing in the
doorway looking inside the room.

                         MANAGER 3
                Here you go gentlemen feel free,
                hope you find what you're looking
                for.

Observing the room turning his head Agent Chase looks at the
Manager of the store.

                         AGENT CHASE
                Thank you for your cooperation.

Turning his head the Manager looks at Agent Chase.

                         MANAGER 3
                No problem.

He walks away from Detective Jones and Agent Chase and
exits. Watching the Manager walk away Agent Chase slowly
turns his head to Detective Jones.

                         AGENT CHASE
                Go get the kid.

After listening to Agent Chase quickly Detective Jones
exits.

INT. BIANCA'S SEXY BOUTIQUE - SECURITY CAMERA ROOM - DAY -
EVENING

Man 4, Agent Chase and Detective Jones are inside the
Security Camera Room looking at the Security footage.

                         MAN 4
                    Wait, pause it.

Detective Jones pauses the video. Staring at the monitor
Man4 points at a freeze frame image of Victoria.

                         MAN 4
                    That's her.

Agent Chase and Detective Jones both looks and stares at the
monitor looking and revealing Victoria's face.

INT./EXT. JANICE'S APARTMENT - DAY - AFTERNOON

Janice hears a knock at the door. She walks to the door and
opens it. Victoria is standing in the doorway. Shock and
amaze to see Victoria grabbing her for a hug Janice smiles.

                         JANICE
                    (Smiles)
                 Vicki.

Embracing Janice's hug standing in the door way Victoria
smiles.

                         VICTORIA
                    (Smiles)
                 Janice.

Still hugging Victoria with her eyes close while smiling a
tear falls down Janice's eye.

                         JANICE
                    (Smiles)
                 It's been a long time.

Pushing away and stops hugging Victoria in a moment of
relief she looks at her and smiles.

                         JANICE
                    (Smiles)
                 Come in.

Victoria walks inside Janice's apartment.

INT. JANICE'S APARTMENT - DAY - AFTERNOON

Janice closes the door. Walking in the living room Victoria
sits on the sofa. Following Victoria into the living room
Janice sits next to her on the sofa.

INT. JANICE'S APARTMENT - LIVING ROOM - DAY - AFTERNOON

Leaning back on the sofa with her arms folded Janice looks
at Victoria.

                    JANICE
          Where have you been, what have you
          been up to?

Taking deep breathes inhaling and exhaling Victoria
gradually looks at Janice.

                    VICTORIA
               (Inhales, Exhales)
          A lot.

Janice side eyes Victoria.

                    VICTORIA
          What?

She looks at Victoria and smiles.

                    JANICE
          It's just so good to see you.

Looking around the living room Victoria smiles picking up a
old photograph of her and Janice on the living room night
stand table.

                    VICTORIA
               (Smiles)
          It's good to be home.

Adjusting her self on the sofa to get more comfortable
Janice unfolds her arms leaning closer to Victoria.

                    JANICE
          I know you're not staying long.

Smirking looking at Janice shrugging her shoulders Victoria
nonchalantly responds.

                    VICTORIA
          I got some business I need to
          handle out here so I'm just
          swinging by.

Squinting her eyes looking at Victoria in a unsure way
Janice hums a noise of disbelief.

                                        (CONTINUED)

                         JANICE
              Just swinging by huh? Uh...huh.

Sitting up raising her body up from the living room sofa
Janice looks down at Victoria and ask.

                         JANICE
              Would you like something to drink?

Watching Janice looking up at her quickly responding
Victoria ask happily.

                         VICTORIA
              Do you have water?

Standing up Janice walks towards the kitchen exiting the
living room.

                         JANICE
              Girl, you know I do. I keep me some
              water.

Janice walks inside the kitchen.

INT. JANICE'S APARTMENT - KITCHEN - DAY - AFTERNOON

                         JANICE
              Have you heard about that crazy
              woman that's been on the News?
              What's that name they call her the
              DB Slasher?

INT. JANICE'S APARTMENT - LIVING ROOM - DAY - AFTERNOON

Victoria answers Janice's question while sitting on the sofa
in the living room.

                         VICTORIA
              Not really just bits and pieces
              about her on what they broadcast on
              the news.

INT. JANICE'S APARTMENT - KITCHEN - DAY - AFTERNOON

Opening the refrigerator Janice grabs two bottles of water.

                         JANICE
              Uh...huh...Do you know if they
              catch her yet?

She closes the refrigerator and exits the kitchen.

INT. JANICE'S APARTMENT - LIVING ROOM - DAY - AFTERNOON

                    VICTORIA
          I don't think so, she seems to
          smart for them to catch her.

Janice walks back to the living room and hands Victoria a
bottle water. Reaching her hand towards the bottle of water
Victoria grabs it from Janice. Sitting down next to Victoria
on the sofa with a bottle of water in her hand Janice sips
the water then place it on the night stand table.

                    JANICE
          She's something to be able to kill
          people for this long. I have been
          following her story for a while
          now, I'm a huge fan. Killing rapist
          and women beaters shit that's
          brilliant these men will know not
          to disrespect any women now,
          because if they do the DB Slasher
          will come and kill, taking that
          little brain they think with the
          fuck off.

Shrugging her shoulders Victoria turns her head and looks at
Janice.

                    VICTORIA
          Yeah I guess.

Side eying Victoria reaching out for her water bottle on the
night stand table grabbing the water bottle Janice leans
back on the sofa for comfort.

                    JANICE
          Uh...huh.

Holding the water bottle next to her sitting on the sofa
Janice removes the bottle top then puts it close to her
mouth.

                    JANICE
          So, what business do you need
          handle out here?

She sips the water watching Victoria give her a evil stare.

                    VICTORIA
          I can't tell you that.

Responding nervously Janice puts the bottle top back on the
water bottle placing it on the night stand table.

(CONTINUED)

                              JANICE
                    Come on we never keep secrets from
                    each other.

Victoria looks at Janice and smiles.

                              VICTORIA
                    Well, there's a first time for
                    everything. I got to go.

Guzzling the water until the bottle is empty while standing
up, placing the bottle on the night stand table Victoria
walks towards the front door. Janice follows Victoria to the
front door.

                              VICTORIA
                    It was good to see you and catch
                    up.

Stretching her arms out to hug Janice a tear falls down
Victoria's right facial cheek. Hugging Janice, closing her
eyes, taking a deep breathe Victoria embraces the moment.

                              VICTORIA
                    I love you and I'm going to miss
                    you.

Holding and hugging Janice tighter with her eyes close
shocking Janice creating a sense of worry Victoria slowly
smiles. Speaking in a nervous tone Janice loosens her grip
on Victoria's back looking at her from the corner of her
eye.

                              JANICE
                    Okay, I love you too sis.

Victoria and Janice stop hugging each other turning away
Victoria reaches out for the front door knob. Grabbing and
turning the door knob Victoria opens the door.

                              VICTORIA
                    Later Sis.

Janice watches Victoria walk and exits the front door.

                              JANICE
                    Later.

Closing the front door Janice sighs.

                              JANICE
                          (Sighs)

INT. POLICE PRECINCT - STAFF BREAK ROOM - DAY - EVENING

Agent Chase is sitting at a table looking and going through
case files. The Forensics Lab tech sees Agent Chase and
approaches him with papers and files in his hands.

                    LAB TECH
          I fucking got it.

Throwing the files on the table in front of him, smiling,
the Lab Tech looks down at Agent Chase nodding his head.
Looking away from the files Agent Chase looks up at the Lab
Tech.

                    AGENT CHASE
          What the fuck, you got?

Sitting down in a chair next to Agent chase opening up the
folder of the files the Lab Tech reveals the DNA results to
Agent Chase.

                    LAB TECH
          I got the I.D of our killer.

He looks at the file reading the information that the Lab
Tech is showing him with excitement.

                    AGENT CHASE
          You're shitting me! Who is it?

Pointing at the name "Victoria Williams" in bold letters and
information that shows the DNA match of the saliva found
from the victim's lip match to the DNA coding of Victoria,
the Lab Tech speaks in a assertive tone.

                    LAB TECH
                 (Assertive Tone)
          Victoria Williams from Myrtle
          Beach, South Carolina.

Agent Chase looks and reads the information grabbing the
file closer to him.

                    AGENT CHASE
          Get the fuck out of here, we got
          her.

EXT./INT. WILLIAMS HOME - DAY - AFTERNOON

Mrs. Williams opens the front door looking back talking to
Mr. Williams.

                    MRS. WILLIAMS
          I'm going to go to the store
          Phillip I'll be back in a hour.

Victoria is standing in the door way.

                    VICTORIA
          Hi Mom.

Turning her head shocked and surprised Mrs. Williams begins
to cry seeing Victoria in the door way. She grabs Victoria
and hugs her tight.

                    MRS. WILLIAMS
                    (Cry)
          Victoria! Baby, you came back home.
          You really came back home. I
          thought I would never see you
          again.

Crying hugging Mrs. Williams smiling joyfully Victoria
breathes softly and slowly.

                    VICTORIA
                    (Cry)
          Yeah, mom I thought real long and
          hard about coming home. I really
          needed to see you and Dad.

Extending her arms out with her right and left hand on
Victoria's shoulder. Staring at Victoria tears continue to
fall down Mrs. Williams face as she stops to cry.

                    MRS. WILLIAMS
          What's wrong baby?

Repeatedly crying Victoria close her eyes, opens them, then
stops crying exhaling.

                    VICTORIA
                    (Exhaling)
          A lot mom, a lot has happen over
          this past year. I just need to be
          with my family at this moment
          that's all.

Wiping the tears off Victoria's face with her hands Mrs.
Williams looks at and hugs Victoria.

(CONTINUED)

                              MRS. WILLIAMS
                    Baby, we are here for you, come in.

Wrapping her right arm around Victoria escorting her inside
the house Mrs. Williams yells.

                              MRS. WILLIAMS
                         (Yells)
                    Philip our baby is home!

INT. WILLIAMS HOME - LIVING ROOM - DAY - AFTERNOON

Mr. Williams is sitting in the living room watching a sport
event on the television.

                              MR. WILLIAMS
                    It's about damn time.

EXT./INT. WILLIAMS HOME - DAY - AFTERNOON

Mrs. Williams closes the front door after Victoria and her
self walks inside the house.

INT. ERIC'S AND VICTORIA'S APARTMENT - DAY - EVENING

Victoria breaks into her old apartment that she shared with
Eric with a huge duffel bag in her hand. Walking around the
vacant apartment Victoria sees rats and roaches crawling all
over the apartment. Touching the walls, cabinets and floors
Victoria reminisces about her relationship with Eric leading
up to murdering him. She sits on the floor in the bedroom
that they shared. Placing her hand in the bag she grab and
pulls out her trophies and lays them on the floor. She
spreads them out making an evil demonic symbol then begins a
demonic ritual.

EXT. ERIC'S AND VICTORIA'S APARTMENT - EVENING - NIGHT

Agent Chase and Detective Jones and other Police officers in
squad cars altogether drives up to Victoria's and Eric's
vacant Apartment with their lights and sirens on. They get
out of their cars running towards the front door of the
apartment with guns in their hands and on their waist.

EXT. / INT. ERIC'S AND VICTORIA'S APARTMENT - EVENING -
NIGHT

Standing at the front door with guns in their hands Agent
Chase yells with Detective Jones standing next to him with
20 to 30 men and women police officers next to and behind
them. Others waiting by the cars with their guns in hands
pointed at the apartment ready to shoot. Stepping to the
side of the front door of the apartment Agent Chase knocks
on it and yells.

Sfx: Door Knocking

                    AGENT CHASE
                (Yells)
            Victoria! This is the FBI! Come out
            with your hands up!

Removing his gun out of his holster with his hand. Holding
and pointing it at the front door of the apartment Agent
Chase yells.

                    AGENT CHASE
                (Yells)
            If you don't come out quietly and
            cooperate with us, we will have to
            use force!

Agent Chase looks at Detective Jones and nods his head,
Detective Jones nods his head back at him. Detective Jones
stands inches away from the door to build up momentum to
kick the door down. He kicks the door busting it open
tearing the hinges apart.

INT. ERIC'S AND VICTORIA'S APARTMENT - EVENING - NIGHT

Walking inside the apartment with their guns in hand
surveying the inside of the apartment Detective Jones, Agent
Chase and other Police Officers stands in a empty living
room.

INT. ERIC'S AND VICTORIA'S APARTMENT - LIVING ROOM - EVENING
- NIGHT

In a pitch black dark room Detective Jones and Agent Chase
hears the door close.

Sfx: Door Squeaking and Slamming Shut loudly

                                            (CONTINUED)

                         DETECTIVE JONES
                    What was that?

Sound of human bodies drop to the floor.

Sfx: Bodies Falling Down to the Floor Rapidly

Pulling out their flashlights Agent Chase and Detective
Jones turns them on. Moving the flashlights around the
apartment they both see dead bodies laying on the floor with
their throats slit surrounding them.

                         AGENT CHASE
                    What the fuck?

Shining the light onto Detective Jones face with his
flashlight holding the gun by his side Agent Chase turns
away from the dead bodies and looks at him.

                         AGENT CHASE
                    Search those rooms while our search
                    these.

Detective Jones nods his head at Agent Chase and proceeds to
walk down the hallway.

INT. VICTORIA AND ERIC'S APARTMENT - HALLWAY - EVENING -
NIGHT

Looking for Victoria in the Kitchen and bathroom Detective
Jones opens and peeks through each door. Agent Chase walks
down the hallway searching for Victoria in the apartments
closets by looking through the crack of the closet doors.
Detective Jones opens the bedroom door and sees her
trophies. Male genitalia/penises hundreds of them laying and
hanging all over the room.

                         DETECTIVE JONES
                    This is some sick shit, all clear.

Jerking his neck preventing himself from vomiting keeping
his lips shut Detective Jones closes the bedroom door.
Walking into the guest room Agent Chase yells.

INT. ERIC'S AND VICTORIA'S APARTMENT - GUEST ROOM - EVENING
- NIGHT

                         AGENT CHASE
                    (Yells)
                    Clear here!

INT. ERIC'S AND VICTORIA'S APARTMENT - HALLWAY - EVENING -
NIGHT

Leaving the guest room Agent Chase walks down the apartment
hallway checking closets. He opens the hallway closet door
Victoria quickly grabs and gags him out of nowhere.
Detective Jones turns the corner into the living room with
his gun in one hand and his flashlight in the other hand.

INT. ERIC'S AND VICTORIA'S APARTMENT - LIVING ROOM - EVENING
- NIGHT

He sees Victoria in the living room standing with her Chef's
knife that's dripping with blood at Agent Chase neck in one
hand and a gun pointed at him in the other.

                    DETECTIVE JONES
              Drop the weapon Victoria.

Standing in front of Victoria with her arm wrapped around
his neck and knife press against it, Agent Chase looks at
Detective Jones and yells.

                    AGENT CHASE
                    (Yells)
              Jones shoot her!

Applying pressure holding the knife tight on his neck in one
hand drawing blood from it, pointing the gun at Detective
Jones with her other hand. She looks at Detective Jones and
calmly speaks.

                    VICTORIA
              Put your gun down.

Shining his flashlight onto her face Detective Jones yells
as his grip tightens onto the gun, pointing it at Victoria.

                    DETECTIVE JONES
                    (Yells)
              Drop your weapon or I will shoot
              you!

Agent Chase stares at Detective Jones with fear in his eyes
and yells.

                    AGENT CHASE
                    (Yells)
              Jones kill her!

Drawing more blood off Agent Chase's neck Victoria applies
more pressure to the knife.

                                        (CONTINUED)

                         VICTORIA
                Put down your gun or I will kill
                him and then you.

Pulling his gun away from Victoria conceding to her request
Detective Jones becomes frustrated.

                     DETECTIVE JONES
                Fine.

Watching Detective Jones bending down, placing the gun down
on the ground Agent Chase begins to sweat nervously with a
tear falling down his right facial cheek.

                       AGENT CHASE
                No Jones don't be stupid.

Detective Jones stands up with his hands up and palms open.

                     DETECTIVE JONES
                What do you want?

Victoria applies more pressure to the knife.

                         VICTORIA
                What every one wants, freedom.

With his arms half way up and hands open towards Victoria's
direction Detective Jones stands and looks at Victoria.

                     DETECTIVE JONES
                I can't do that.

Staring deeply into Detective Jones' eyes with a evil grin
Victoria calmly speaks.

                         VICTORIA
                If you don't, he dies.

Looking at Victoria pointing at a wall Detective Jones
smirks.

                     DETECTIVE JONES
                There are tons of cops out there
                waiting for you and willing to
                shoot and kill you at any moment.
                How are you going to get pass them?

She glances at Agent Chase and smiles, then looks at
Detective Jones giggling.

(CONTINUED)

>   VICTORIA
>   (Smiles and Giggles)
>   I'll take my chances.

Slitting Agent Chase throat Victoria fires a gun shot at
Detective Jones.

Sfx: Gun Shot

Falling down to the ground, maneuvering, and dodging the
bullets missing Detective Jones completely. He quickly grabs
the gun off the floor standing and pointing it at Victoria.
Putting his index finger on the trigger he fires a gun shot
at Victoria.

Sfx: Gun Shot

Hitting her in the chest the impact force her to fall
backwards pulling down Agent Chase with her to the floor.
Running to Agent Chase, seeing a cloth on the ground next to
him, picking it up, placing it on the cut, and around Agent
Chase's neck/throat. Putting his hands on top of Agent
Chase's neck Detective Jones applies pressure on the cut to
stop it from bleeding. Police officers storm into the
apartment seeing Victoria lying on the floor with a gun and
knife in her hands. Next to Detective Jones applying
pressure with his hands on top of a cloth on Agent Chase's
neck/throat.

INT. (PRESENT) WOMEN'S PRISON VISITING/INTERVIEW ROOM - DAY
- AFTERNOON

Sitting across from Detective Jones with shackles and
handcuffs on her wrist and ankles Victoria has a nonchalant
look on her face.

>   VICTORIA
>   Now you know the whole story, can I
>   go now Detective.

Detective Jones shakes his head with a disappointing look on
his face.

>   DETECTIVE JONES
>   Joshua said, you were evil.

Slamming her fists on the table Victoria speaks in an
aggressive tone.

>   VICTORIA
>   (Aggressive Tone)

>   (MORE)

                         VICTORIA (cont'd)
              Pain and trauma created me. The
              people who caused that pain need to
              feel that pain they have caused.

Yelling with aggression Detective Jones stares at Victoria.

                         DETECTIVE JONES
                         (Yells)
              What about Chase and the other
              officers you've killed that night?

Laughing at Detective Jones rolling her eyes Victoria looks
and responds calmly.

                         VICTORIA
              You all were in my way. And to add,
              you came looking for me.

Jumping out of his seat standing to his feet Detective Jones
stares and yells.

                         DETECTIVE JONES
                         (Yells)
              Because, you're a killer!

Victoria moves her head left to right speaking with an
aggressive tone.

                         VICTORIA
              No, I'm a victim. I just decide to
              let justice be by my hands instead
              of yours.

She turns her head and looks at the Correctional
Officer/Prison Guard.

                         VICTORIA
              Guard, I'm ready to go back to my
              cell now. Me and the Detective are
              done here.

Correctional Officer/Prison Guard approaches Victoria lifts
her off the chair, then begins to escort her out of the
interview room. Sitting in his his chair Detective Jones
watches the Correctional Officer/Prison Guard and Victoria
leave the room.

                         DETECTIVE JONES
              Yes we are.

                                              (CONTINUED)

Standing by her left and right shoulder one guard on the
left and the other guard on the right escorting Victoria out
of the room. Detective Jones cell phone rings, quickly he
answers the phone sitting in the chair.

>

                    DETECTIVE JONES
          Yeah.

                                              INTER CUT

INT. HOSPITAL - DAY - AFTERNOON

With a bandage wrapped around his neck Agent Chase is laying
down on the bed with a heart monitor beeping and IV fluid
bag hanging next to him.

                    AGENT CHASE
          You still talking to Coo, Coo.

Getting out of the chair Detective Jones begins to leave the
interview/Visiting room.

                    DETECTIVE JONES
          We just wrapped up. How are you?

Sitting up on the hospital bed Agent Chase relaxes watching
the nurse walk in checking the heart monitor and the fluid
in the IV bag.

                    AGENT CHASE
          I'm getting better. Hey Jones I
          never thank you for saving my life.

                                              INTER CUT

INT. WOMEN'S PRISON - VISITING/INTERVIEW ROOM - DAY -
AFTERNOON

Detective Jones exits the interview room/Visiting room.

INT. WOMEN'S PRISON - HALLWAY - DAY - AFTERNOON

He walks down the hallway toward the exit doors.

                    DETECTIVE JONES
          You're my partner, I always got
          your back.

                                              INTER CUT

INT. HOSPITAL - DAY - AFTERNOON

Holding the phone to his ear Agent Chase smiles.

                    AGENT CHASE
                  (Smiles)
            You damn right, partner. Hey maybe
            I can get you a job in the Bureau.

Approaching the exit doors Detective Jones smiles.

                    DETECTIVE JONES
                  (Smiles)
            I think about it. Take care Chase.

Exiting the Prison doors Detective Jones continues to smile.
Agent Chase leans his head back on the pillow and smiles.

                    AGENT CHASE
                  (Smiles)
            You too Jones.

They both hangs up their phones ending the call.

INT. WOMEN'S PRISON - HALLWAY - DAY - AFTERNOON

Victoria is being escorted back to her cell with
Correctional Officers surrounding her. They stop walking she
looks out the prison window and see a crowd of women
chanting "DB slasher" with signs in their hands saying "Free
the DB Slasher". She looks closely and sees Janice in the
crowd chanting and smiling. The Correctional officers and
Victoria proceeds to walk.

EXT. WOMEN'S PRISON - DAY - AFTERNOON

Janice is chanting DB slasher and free DB slasher repeatedly
with a group of women. Mr. and Mrs. Williams walks into the
crowd hand in hand standing next to Janice chanting with
her. They look at Janice chanting and yelling. She looks at
them and together they turn their heads towards the Prison
building chanting.

                    THE END

                                        FADE OUT

Credits

Made in United States
Orlando, FL
29 January 2022